OCCULT
MALIGNANCY

A Novel

JAMES STEELE, MD

Occult Malignancy

Copyright © 2021 by James Steele, MD

Published by
Illumify Media Global
www.IllumifyMedia.com
"Let's bring your book to life!"

Library of Congress Control Number: 2021920633

Paperback ISBN: 978-0-9987896-8-2

Typeset by Art Innovations (http://artinnovations.in/)
Cover design by Debbie Lewis

Printed in the United States of America

"Well, glory hallelujah, I raise my glass up to you.
And bow my head with utmost respect.
But I think it's only fair to warn you,
There's a storm and it's coming up on you.
And like the wind and the rain, my words are direct."

—C. and R. Robinson

Occult (*adjective*): not revealed, secret; not manifest or detectable by clinical methods alone

Malignancy (*noun*): exhibition (as by a tumor) of malignant qualities; virulence

CHAPTER ONE

EDGAR WAS SITTING at the counter of his usual diner sipping coffee. He was in every morning, around this time. The waitress behind the counter knew him well. He had been in the insurance business for years. Sales, new policies. Auto, life, home. He had been single his entire adult life and had no children. Because of this, he had been eligible for retirement early. Qualified at only fifty-five years of age. But he enjoyed the work too much, the people, the interactions. So he stayed on with the company, and almost another fifteen years had passed. He had invested and saved well, so working long hours had been a thing of the past. He was practically part-time now. He took his time with new customers as well as those with whom he had longtime relationships. His door-to-door sales style had afforded him many strong ties to this community that he loved so much. Edgar was close with Jim Clarkson, the bank manager at Glendale Savings and Loan, where he had been banking for at least two decades.

Edgar spent little on personal extravagance. His car was an early model 1989 Subaru Baja, which he maintained himself and fixed up with parts from the Leetsdale Auto Parts store. His friend Nate

Bickers owned the store. Edgar had sold him a life insurance policy ten years ago.

Katie, the waitress behind the counter, held up the coffee pot and raised her eyebrows at Edgar. He smiled and said, "Please," and then looked back down at the *Post*. Woody Paige was ripping the Broncos' front office as usual for not spending more money on available free agents. It had been several years now since John Elway had won back-to-back Super Bowls, and the city was getting antsy for another successful football season. Edgar made pleasantries with some of the other customers at the counter of Sam's Number 3 Diner. He knew most of the regulars and had sold some of them various policies over the years.

Katie filled two of their cups, then meandered back to Edgar's stool. "Whatcha up to today, Ed? I know you're not off to work," she threw in with a wink. His "part-time" status was a long-running joke.

Edgar took a sip of the steaming joe and said, "Well, I guess I have a little puttering to do around the house today."

"Sounds exciting," she added as she sauntered away.

Edgar just smiled. After another twenty minutes of chitchatting, finishing the *Post*, discussing the weather, Edgar paid his check, left a 30 percent tip for Katie, and headed out toward his Baja. He had a few errands to run before heading back to his small ranch house on Holly Street in south Denver.

CHAPTER TWO

A CAREER in health care oftentimes means that your life, your rhythm is simply out of sync with the rest of America, the rest of the world. My name is Michael Schwartz. I was employed as a hospitalist physician at a major metro medical center in downtown Denver. As you learn, hospitals do not close. Holidays become essentially meaningless. Weekends lose value. "Nine to five" is just a movie from the eighties with Dolly Parton.

Our lives are either shift based or day based. You leave home before your kids are awake, and you return home, if you are lucky, before their bedtime. The grass is always greener; whatever you are doing, it's not enough. Consumed by work, I was a part-time husband and father. Though only thirteen years into my career, it felt much longer. Much more time missed. Away from home . . . always at work. I had tried to be there for my wife and kids but fell short. Now on my own again, Denver seemed like a good place to settle in. I had bounced around a little before returning to my hometown. The divorce had been quick if not completely painless. I had felt like I was doing the best I could, but sometimes when we health care folks choose our patients over our families enough times, one day we lose one side. I feel no ill will toward my ex. She'd moved to Los

Angeles. She'd met someone and was now raising our kids on the West Coast. Personally, I felt that the mountains of Colorado were a superior place to rear children, but my say in such matters was moot these days. The Rockies are better when you have someone to share them with, I had learned, so I threw myself back into work and rarely ventured to the mountains as a result.

So, there I was, making rounds at work and in my own life, by myself. Could have been worse. I missed my kids, though. When I was a fourth-year medical student, I was on surgical rotation in New York. The residents were hard, tough, and unrelenting. I was rarely up to speed with them, and I heard about it often. "I don't know who you're rounding on every day, Schwartz, but this guy looks like he's gonna fucking die. Get your shit together." I guess I figured I was just reporting the facts to my superiors. Their opinion was, *Figure it out, fix it, save the fucking guy. Make us look good.* I learned quickly. By the end of the rotation I was ordering and drawing my own labs, conducting radiology studies, calling consults, and starting meds. I realized I had a knack. Once, my senior resident was so exhausted, she passed out in the call room. I could not find her or wake her. Her pager must have died. I managed the service for a whole shift, prevented a fifty-six-year-old lady from going blind from something called temporal arteritis, and realized that I could do this. Internal medicine was a better fit, so I made a career of it.

I was born and raised in Denver. I went to elementary school and junior high here. But we moved away around maybe ninth grade. When the tragedy happened to my family, we left. In any case, I was ten years post residency, and I was now back. Unfinished business perhaps.

My parents were dead. My marriage had ended. My ex and I had lived in Chicago, Austin, Savannah. None of those cities made her happy. Maybe SoCal would. Me, I needed the mountains again. By this point in my career, I had become very proficient and efficient in hospital medicine. I was what they call a hospitalist. This is an in-patient medical physician. We don't have offices or exam rooms in some office building somewhere. We see only hospitalized patients and spend 100 percent of our work time within the walls of a hospital. Most of our patient load comes from the emergency room. An ER doctor calls with a patient for admission, we go to evaluate the patient, and decide upon a treatment for him or her. Usual cases involve the elderly with multiple chronic illnesses and some acute ones. We treat the acuity as best we can. Diagnoses include pneumonia in a patient with bad lungs already. That patient's primary care physician has been trying to treat his long-standing COPD, also called emphysema. Eventually he ends up in the ER. I order antibiotics, breathing treatments, incentive spirometry, mucolytics, for example, to try to break up the mucous-based, pus-filled lungs and improve the oxygenation so that the patient feels better. Then he goes home. And sees his primary care doc. And it all starts over again. The administrators want him in the hospital for fewer than three days. It's my job to make sure that happens. With a smile on my face so that the patient feels he had a great experience from my service in my hospital. I call myself a maître d' of a fast-food restaurant.

I want you in.

I want you taken care of.

I want you satisfied.

I want you out.

So that's how it went. For every twelve hours of work, I was off for twelve hours. For every week of work, I was off for a week. Not a bad deal really. Long days, long weeks. Then, one that flew by. I would try to see the kids as much as possible during my off week. They were both enrolled in private school somewhere in LA County. Progressive, British something or other. The grades were combined. Kindergarten, first, and second all together, then third, fourth, and fifth. Like that. My kids were six and eight years old, respectively. First and third grades. My ex was happy. Of course she was. I was paying for all of this. A divorced man splitting time between Denver and Los Angeles. Two of the most expensive markets in the country. The travel was expensive. The recession of 2008 was over. Things were starting to pick up. Obama had just been elected to his second term last November. To pay for this sudden two-city lifestyle I had been thrust into, I was picking up extra work in my week off sometimes. It paid more to work in underserved areas like western Colorado or New Mexico. I could double my salary by just picking up a few shifts in those places. A rural hospital. They were always in need, and it felt nice to be needed. The paychecks didn't hurt either. By the time I was in my midthirties, I was working about twenty to twenty-two days a month. One long weekend a month was usually all I got to see my kids most months, sometimes not at all. I thought about just moving to SoCal and finding work there. I just could not leave Denver. I told myself the mountains were in my blood. But there were other things holding me back. Keeping me here.

I could have fought harder for more visitation. I could have fought for primary custody. The truth was, I was not the world's greatest father. I just was not. I would try to do the dad things: playing in the park, horseback riding lessons, Legoland. It just did not click. They wanted to be with their mom, and I wanted them to be happy. As strange as it sounds, I was alone so much, I forgot how to be social. I did not relate to the kids very well. I just didn't have it. I worked hard. I paid for their apartment, school, vacations, clothes, toys. Other than financially, I just was not much of a figure in their lives. It silently ate at me. I wished it were different. I was not what you think of when you think of Dad. I was a doctor. The truth was, my ex and I never actually sat down and divided our assets. That was just money that went straight to the lawyers, which I detested. So, we signed papers, I agreed to pay for everything child related, and she could have her divorce, free to move on to smoggier pastures. That did not bother me really. I personally had little interest in meeting someone new. She would most likely be remarried within a year or two. I was worried that she would be meeting some SoCal douchebag. Lance or Steven or Jack or whoever the fuck it was going to be might have asked her to make my child support fully legal, but then he could pay for the fees that went along with that. She ended up meeting a good guy, though. He was good to the kids, and he was glad I was rarely around. I kept paying for everything. There was nothing in writing that stated I was required to do it. I just liked to. For the time being. I thought there was a Cold War term called mutually assured destruction to this arrangement. As long as my ex didn't complain, I would keep paying. If she started to press, I would stop.

When I was still a family man, and was setting up my/our will and trust some months or years back, my attorney mentioned something to me. He was a dad as well, about my age. He seemed like a good guy, and he was drafting the whole will and estate deal for a trade. "Normally, I'd charge you fifteen hundred bucks for this," he said. "But I really like that leather Restoration Hardware sofa you have in your living room. They don't make that one anymore. I checked." His large frame leaned back in his chair so that it squeaked. "I'd like to put it in my man cave so I can watch the Irish on it on Saturdays." A devoted Notre Dame alum. They all were. "You get it over to my house and we'll call the whole thing even." A sly smile crept onto his face.

So clever, I thought. He could give a shit about my family's welfare. He wanted the damn couch so he could park his fat ass on it. He was clearly taking advantage of the fact that I had been purging anything in my house that my ex, Shannon, had left behind when she left for LA. My quick-witted barrister Doug and his wife, Stephanie, had been to our house a few times. He had commented on our leather couch on more than one occasion. It probably wasn't worth fifteen hundred dollars anyway. I had stained a corner cushion when our beagle, Lester, had vomited on it and I used Fantastik cleaning spray to try to wipe up bits of Pupperoni and feces he had consumed on a leashless walk a few hours earlier.

To add to my indignity, I would also have to schlep this leather beast over to Doug's house. I would have to borrow a pickup from someone. This deal seemed about even. Shannon would likely end up with the money anyway in some form if it did not go to Doug. Then, at least I'd have a will and trust for my kids.

"Consider it done," I said to Doug. "It will be there Friday." I figured that I would pay my neighbor Jeff's kid Jackson fifty bucks either to help me with his pickup or maybe to do the job himself. He was a good kid. He was taking a gap year between high school and college and was home quite a bit. I was not really sure what "gap year" meant anyway. I barely had a "gap" half hour these days. I suppose if someone is letting you sponge off them rent free, more power to you. "Anything else, counselor?" I began to zip up my black North Face backpack as I stood.

"Yep. One other thing." Doug leaned forward again. He flipped through some pages on his messy desk. "Trust. Your estate, in the event of your death, should be in a trust of some kind." He slipped on some readers. He was switching back from college football fan to lawyer. "As in, you are leaving everything to the kids. Mostly life insurance if you die, but also your house, car, etc. Makes sense. But if they're still minors when you pass, Shannon can petition to have the funds go to her. And if she's remarried by then, this new man can be added to said petition." It had not occurred to me that Shannon would marry this guy. I guess I knew very little of her plans, but it didn't really matter to me.

"I hadn't thought of that, Doug, but I get what you're saying about the new person in her life. I need to protect the kids from their mother and her decisions." It occurred to me then how complicated divorce really is. I had made this appointment with Doug because I did not want Shannon to get and keep all of the money earmarked for the kids in the event of my death. Now it seemed I had to protect her and them from whoever she moved on with, as this person would likely not have their best interests at heart. The "future suitors," as it read in the trust agreement, may choose to take advantage. In light of a used couch, it looked like I was getting very valuable legal advice.

"Yeah, man," he continued, "I have a trust with my sister as trustee." His sister was a drunk and a neighborhood gossip, but that wasn't my concern. "You need to appoint a trustee who will look after the kids' interests."

I thought about this. I didn't like many of my options. My parents were dead. I had had one sister; she was also dead. I couldn't ask any of my old college buddies; too much time had passed. "Shannon's mother, Peggy." It came out before I'd processed it. "She'd always liked me better anyway. And she loves those kids. She'll look out for them."

Doug filled in some lines of the contract. "Done," he said. "I'll forward her a copy."

"Great. Thanks, Doug. That couch will be in your den by the time College GameDay opens in South Bend this Saturday."

"Go Irish," he said as he walked out of the office.

CHAPTER THREE

SO, with my children's financial future seemingly tucked in for the time being, I found myself back at work the next day. I was waiting for a chart at the 3C nurses' station, a general medical-surgical unit. The typical stomping ground for a hospitalist. A family trudged past me. Two adults, a teenager pushing a very old man in a wheelchair. He looked like an exhumed corpse. He was covered from the waist down in an old blanket. The foursome entered room 315 across from the nurses' station. About five minutes later, I was finishing my note in the chart I'd been waiting for, now documenting how my COPD patient in room 317 was slow to make progress. At only age forty-eight, she would be on oxygen for the rest of her life. And that life had maybe ten years left on it. Them cigarettes. I left out my commentary in my note, of course, but that was the real medical assessment of the patient.

"Continue steroids at current dose. Solumedrol 60 mg IV Q6 (every six) hours. Albuterol/Atrovent nebulizer every four hours scheduled, six hours as needed. Deescalate antibiotics to cover for atypical organisms. Consider pulmonary medicine consult tomorrow if no improvement with wheezes and oxygenation."

A pulmonologist would have nothing else to add, as I knew from working with our in-house lung specialist, Dr. King, for four years of doing this job. With him around, it would make my patient feel like I was pulling out all the stops if I consulted. So I did just that. Something we do in medicine. A lot.

The teenager from room 315 wheeled her grandpa out of the room and approached me at the counter. I guess, with some semblance of a shirt and tie I looked doctor-y enough for a medical question.

A dermatologist I knew from Texas had a standard line to the question, "Doc, what is this on my arm?" He'd look it over and say without changing expression, "That is . . . about seventy-five dollars. Book an appointment." I always loved that line. These folks seemed a bit more apprehensive and were, of course, my patient's family, so I'd be a bit more polite.

"Can you help my great grandpa?" she said. "He's sick." I closed the three-ring binder of a chart I was writing in and set it back on the rack.

"What's going on with him?" I asked, worried I would not be able to help much from this hallway other than give some advice.

"He's got a bladder infection, I think," she proffered.

"Oh, I see," I replied. "Did he say it's uncomfortable when he urinates?" I was trying to maintain his dignity as best I could with a quiet voice, but space was limited in the small hallway.

"No," she said. "His catheter is dirty. It needs to be changed."

"Oh, okay, we may be able to help you with that." I looked up from my stance over the man in the chair and motioned for Lindsey, the charge nurse, to head over to me. For anyone else, she would have shot an "I don't have time for this" glance. But Lindsey liked me. I was a huge advocate for nurses with hospital administration. Nurses and schoolteachers are the two most neglected professions. Underpaid and underappreciated. The world simply could not run without either one, and they get very little acknowledgment.

Lindsey and I bent down to pull back the man's blanket and take a look at the man's Foley catheter and gravity bag. What we found was a total shock and an absolute first for me in this game. The bag was half-full of very dark, yellow urine. Not shocking by itself. But the urine had what I would call no fewer than one hundred cock-roaches swimming in it. They were in the liquid, on the surface, on the bag walls, and, most concerning, crawling up the tubing into his penis and urethra. My stomach dropped like I was on an airplane that just plunged about a thousand feet unexpectedly during some turbulence. I felt a twinge of vomit in my throat. I had to remain stoic, as all health care professionals do. Lindsey pretended like she saw a hundred of these a day.

"Let's get Great Grandpa downstairs to the ER. We can get his Foley out and get him all cleaned up. Why don't you go grab Mom and Dad and let them know we'll be taking him down now?"

Within a few minutes we were in a curtained room in the ER deflating the balloon and removing the catheter. The plan was to get this entire bag to microbiology in an effort to identify any and all bacterial presence in the urine. My buddy Jeremy Weinstock was a urologist. He was going to have to take this poor old guy to cystoscopy and clean out his bladder and ureters. I would later find out that there were twenty-three roaches up there. One was trying to get into the guy's left kidney. All were removed, and with strong IV antibiotics this man would be able to go home in about a week.

You ask how this could happen to a person. Living in America. But people just do not know. Grandpa seems fine, leave him be. People distrust hospitals and doctors. I do not always blame them. This is why I have a job and have managed to do very well in it. It is why I have two kids at a very expensive private school in Los Ange-les. Because sooner or later, everyone ends up in the emergency room.

CHAPTER FOUR

AS EDGAR PULLED into the Home Depot parking lot in Glendale, Colorado, he pushed up the visor shade on the driver side of his yellow Baja. In the morning, visibility is practically impossible in the Denver area. Now about ten a.m., he was finally facing west. He found a spot in the corner of the lot. Near the Whole Foods. Maybe he would pick up some chicken salad for lunch. If they had the classic version. Not a fan of the kind with grapes or nuts. Plus, lately they had seemed to be making up the weight with more mayonnaise and less chicken. Typical of big corporations, always looking for ways to screw you over.

Anyway, he focused back on his Home Depot errand. He had a great deal to do today. The basement of his Holly Street house needed repairs. Edgar was getting a bit old and arthritic these days, especially for this type of manual labor. Certainly, hiring a handyman was out of the question, however. That would be a big loose end he could not afford. Edgar walked from the Baja to the sliding door marked ENTRANCE. Near it were several young men loitering. Likely illegals from Mexico or Central America looking for day work. "That could possibly work," Edgar thought. Hire one of the men for the day, then take care of him afterward. But if he had any close amigos or *hermanos* with him, maybe even an *esposa* or *hijo*, that would be more loose ends. When the young man failed to show up at Home Depot tomorrow, the family may start asking questions. At the same time, they may just assume that ICE nabbed him, placed him in a detention center somewhere. Edgar was sure that type of thing happened all the time. If it did, he may still be in the clear. Okay, now that settled it. This outing, Edgar would attempt the repairs himself. If he was unsuccessful, next time he would pick up a strapping young caballero and have him complete the work for him. Then adios. Edgar had "adiosed" people before. People who had gotten in the way or knew too much.

The tiling in the nursey was starting to peel and crack. The reinforcement bolt on the door to the room was loosening. It needed to be tightened or simply replaced. The caulking around the sink was fraying also. This could lead to a leak or a breach in the plumbing, which would then spill over outside. While she had not shown any signs of trying to escape in years, it was possible that she was biding her time. Like the Wicked Witch from *The Wizard of Oz*. She was trying to be patient until she could strike. Edgar was always suspicious of his guests. His girls. Even from way back when. Of course, he himself had also spent a great deal of time in a nursery when he was a child. His brother and sister too. Daddy would get upset and punish them. Sometimes separately, sometimes together. In there. Even as a small boy, Edgar (little Eddie then) knew there was no sense in screaming. Daddy had built the nursery and cellar himself. Thick masonry bricks and cement. It was practically a bomb shelter as if from the Cold War. That was what Daddy wanted the neighbors to think anyway. Edgar was walking down aisle 23 of Home Depot, the lumber aisle. He needed to compose himself a bit. The memories of Daddy hurting him that way made his arthritic knees buckle a bit, and tears collected in the edges of his eyes. He did not want to remember that now. It must have been the smell of the fresh lumber and sawdust. That and Daddy's whiskey breath and body odor. He was usually foul smelling while he was teaching the children their lessons.

Edgar was not a monster like Daddy. He had hardly ever hit any of his girls. At age sixty-four his parts did not work as well as they once did. Sometimes he couldn't get hard or hard enough. That reminded him, he needed a new plunger. Or at least a replacement handle from aisle 3. His was worn, and she had gotten a splinter from it last time. Then she cried more than usual. The paint had chipped on it too. A plastic one would be better this time. So after his visits to aisles 23, 17, 3, and 4, Edgar pushed his orange plastic cart to the self-checkout aisle. Loved, loved, loved the self-checkout. No one asking questions, no small talk. Small talk led to mistakes and loose ends. Sure, he always chatted with Katie at the coffee shop. But he was always in character there. Full-fledged acting mode. Edgar the kindly insurance salesman. Sometimes he was even there shopping for new girls.

His total was $181.58. A small price to pay for a nursey repair where one would not hear anything suspicious. Edgar grinned at himself for his foresight—his understanding of his craft and how he was always one step ahead of everyone. As he sauntered back to his yellow Baja, he nodded to the gents at the parking lot edge. Edgar even yelled, "Hasta luego!" to the group, as he figured he might need one of them soon. If today's repairs did not go well, he would need a stronger back to get the work done. For a second Edgar almost felt badly. One last labor gig and this young man would be eventually found in the foothills near Morrison where Edgar typically disposed of his aftermath. If Edgar could soundproof the room himself, maybe the *joven* would be spared. Edgar picked up the pace in the parking lot. He had a great deal to do and wanted to get started. He did not notice at first that his left leg started to drag slightly and felt a little numb.

CHAPTER FIVE

MY NEW ADMISSION was getting settled in his room just past the telemetry monitors on the cardiac unit. His name was Jimmy. He was ninety-two years old. I had seen him briefly in the ER when he first arrived complaining of shortness of breath. Worse when he walked with his walker and worse at night. He had told the triage nurse that he needed three pillows to prop himself up at night in his bed. His symptoms were getting worse over the last few weeks despite taking all his medications the doctor at the VA had prescribed. Jimmy had come in by ambulance from the veterans' home. He had outlived his wife and all of his other family members except for one daughter, with whom he was not close. She lived somewhere in New Mexico now. Jimmy did not approve of her first husband, not a nice man, Jimmy would tell me. Left it at that. Anyway, Jimmy had not spoken with her in twenty years. He knew she was still alive because Jimmy had received a court summons a few months ago looking for her. A bill collection or something like that. Must have been a big bill.

As a general rule, I love veterans. They are my favorite patients. They are a mess medically speaking, however. They've smoked and drunk and been exposed to chemicals and artillery and combat and been essentially treated like shit by our government for years and years. They've protected us and defended us and returned home and received little support while the rest of us are allowed to go to school and get jobs and get rich. Completely unfair. It infuriates me, actually. So I figured the least I could do is sit and listen.

Jimmy had congestive heart failure. A series of heart attacks and a lifetime of smoking had weakened his heart muscle so much that it barely pumped anymore. I knew Jimmy very well. He was here every month or so. Jimmy was what we call a DNR/DNI (Do Not Resuscitate/Do Not Intubate) and had been playing with house money for years. He knew this. He'd get symptomatic and the vet home would call EMS for a ride to the hospital. "The nurses are prettier at the hospital," he'd tell me. Jimmy was a Marine. Not a "former Marine," a Marine. All Marines are Marines for life. They do not lose the title simply because they retire or are discharged or killed. I have been told this many times.

I took a listen to Jimmy's chest with my stethoscope. Years of Allman Brothers Band concerts have left me harder of hearing than I should be at age forty-two. It is what it is. Dickey Betts used to turn his amp up so loud in the nineties. It was painful to the eardrums, and my head would ring for three days after each show. I was not smart enough to wear earplugs then. Anyway . . . another life.

Jimmy's chest sounded wet, though. We say the lungs are full of crackles. His were like Rice Krispies in milk at his lung bases. I asked the nurse to push sixty milligrams of furosemide through Jimmy's IV to help him breathe. His kidneys were also fairly shot. So the medication would be of little help if at all. Lasix works in the kidney. "Do you want us to put in a catheter, Jimmy?" I asked him. "It will sting a bit but it will help get the urine out of your bladder more easily."

"I know, doc. Ain't my first rodeo. Yeah, put it in please," he says reluctantly. Jimmy was dying. He knew this.

I wanted to take Jimmy's mind off the catheter that was about to be inserted into his penis. I knew that each breath was a struggle, but

I said anyway, "Tell me a story, Jimmy. A battle story. One they should make a movie about."

Jimmy let out a sigh as Jenn, the charge nurse, slid in the lubricated catheter tip and dark yellow urine is freed into the tube.

"Doc, I'll tell you a story about the best shot of whiskey I ever had. It was 1944. We had been slugging it out with the Japs on Okinawa for a couple of months. Every single guy I left home with two years prior had been killed by then. I was a corporal at age twenty-four. I had been lucky. My platoon was backed up to the beachfront one day. MacArthur had sent a new fleet to back us up, and they were getting ready to unleash hell. The three-foot cannons —that's diameter, doc, not length—were sounding alarm and preparing to fire on the bluff where most of the Jap positions were. They knew the barrage was coming, so they figured they would try to take as many of us out as they could beforehand. Hirohito had ordered five hundred kamikazes into the fray. It was going to be some battle." Jimmy stopped to take a breath. The Lasix was helping, his lungs were becoming clearer. About a liter of urine had entered the Foley bag. Oxygen saturation was reading 87 percent on the monitor. I was okay with that.

"Just as the USS McKinley fired three rounds, I took a bullet to the thigh by a charging Jap infantryman. I lunged left and clocked him with my left fist and drove my knife right into his chest. He died with a gasp. I was in real trouble, though. I fell to the sand. My leg was bleeding pretty good. The order was coming through from my sergeant to evac the beach because shells were inbound. I couldn't stand or walk very well on my shot-up leg. A corpsman saw me and grabbed a buddy. They got me on a stretcher and began wading out into the sea. A small patrol boat was circling with a medic in it. The three of 'em poured me into that boat." Jimmy paused again. "I found out later that both of the corpsmen bought it shortly after." Another pause. "I asked the medic if he had anything for pain as we sputtered along toward the nearest battleship. He said all I have is this. And he pulled out a beat-up flask and poured me a double shot of Kentucky bourbon. It tasted like maple syrup going down and took the pain away from my leg. I'll tell you, doc, you got anything like that here, I'll take two." He smiled and continued, "I was loaded onto the deck of the McKinley with a series of pulleys. It took twenty minutes to get me up there from the waterline. From the deck, I could see the battle on the beach. It was touch-and-go, for sure. They got me down to sick bay. Foul smelling, boys screaming and dying, blood everywhere. I closed my eyes and tried to get some sack time. My leg hurt less, and the bleeding had slowed. No sooner had I shut my eyelids as the ship's alarm started going off. A kamikaze had hit the stern, and the boat was going down. I looked at the poor fellow next to me, he had a head wound. We knew we would never survive an abandoned ship. So, we made our peace and stayed put. Let 'em help the ones who can be saved, we tried to tell ourselves.

"An hour later, the 'all clear' alarm sounded. The engineers had been able to patch the stern. A medic came by to see me shortly later and took the bullet out of my leg and cleaned the wound and stitched it." Jimmy showed me the scar on his thigh. "Five days later I was on a beach in Hawaii. There were nurses there. Pretty as the ones you have here, doc. I hadn't even seen a woman in over a year. They tried to rehab my leg, but something about the nerve damage, they said I couldn't fight no more. So, six months later I was back in Delta, Colorado, my hometown. And now here I am. Still kickin'," he said with a wink. "But I'll never forget that whiskey, doc."

I was completely dumfounded. I did not know what to say. I usually complain if the coffee's bad. Pathetic.

We diuresed Jimmy as best we could for the next two days in the cardiac unit. He put out over three liters of urine in that time. It was clear, however, he was not going to get any better. He decided on hospice, and we made him as comfortable as we could. I tried to reach his daughter in New Mexico, outside of Santa Fe, but failed. I even called the local police there to try to track her down. No one knew where she was.

Her father, the hero, died alone in our hospital. He survived countless battles in the South Pacific and even a bullet to the thigh, but in the end CHF, or congestive heart failure, caught up with him. We all die of something. The nurses said kind words about him when he passed. His funeral would be a small affair.

CHAPTER SIX

MELISA STRUGGLED TO STAY AWAKE. She did not remember the last time she had eaten. Her water pitcher had been dry for hours. The sick bastard had not bothered to refill it in at least a day. Melisa had been sparing with her ration, a lesson she had learned well over the last few years. She had lost count of the times she had nearly died from dehydration. He was smart. Even when Melisa was younger, maybe fourteen or fifteen, he would wait for her to be weak and dry to do some of his sickest shit. She would be curled up on the floor in a corner when he would come in. She did not even hear him enter the room, and then he would be inside her. Thrusting, grunting, sweating. She was too emaciated to fight him. He would finish in her. On her sometimes. He would put it back inside. It hurt. She hated him. He would crawl off her. She could hear him buckling his pants, his belt. If he had worn his goddamn button-fly slacks, this could take several minutes. Then he would fill her pitcher with ice water, drop off some bread, a banana, a chicken breast, and leave. He would lock the padlock on the outside. The door was sealed. She had been lying there for a moment, composing herself as she sobbed. Then she would sip the water. It was almost like an hourglass. When the pitcher was empty, and she was wasted again, he'd slip back in and it would start all over. It was more and more difficult to tell nightmares from reality.

————

Melisa would force herself to stay awake. She would pull out her own nose hairs sometimes. This hurt and made her sneeze. It bought her a few minutes sometimes. This time she heard the padlock shackle pop open. She heard the keys rattle. She knew he was back from his morning jaunt. The light from the bare bulb in the basement filled the room as the door crept open. He was carrying something. It looked like a small bat. She scurried to the deepest corner of the basement and pulled her knees to her chest as he approached.

Without a word, he swung hard from her left side and struck her in the head. Total blackness. Melisa woke up to find herself duct-taped to a chair with tape over her mouth as well. She could feel a large dirty rag stuffed inside her mouth, almost back to her throat. She felt like she was going to throw up. She writhed in pain. Head was pounding, eyes watering. She could make out her "Daddy," as he called himself, applying some white glue or paste to the corners of the room. The edges near the door. He then fastened board and brackets to the spaces he was working on.

"You're getting louder as you're growing into a woman," he said without looking in her direction. "No more little girl. Someone might hear you. We can't have that." He looked at her and winked. He spoke confidently, but he seemed to be having a little trouble with his manual labor. His left arm seemed to be hanging like a salami in a window. Daddy approached her.

"Now, young lady, I'm going to loosen your tape. Enough for you to wiggle out of while I leave. When you start screaming, I'll know if the new reinforcement and soundproofing is effective. As a reminder of my power, I'm going to give you a little warning first, though." He pushed the chair onto its side on the ground so she was in a fetal position, still bound to the chair, on the filthy basement floor.

He pulled down his shorts and applied some Vaseline to her

backside. He then showed her his new bathroom plunger. The same one he would hit her with. It was plastic and thick. He slowly inserted it into her bottom. Just an inch or two. She winced through her tape gag.

"If you act out, behave with bad manners, this will go in up to the rubber part." He placed the plunger on her lap. The white plastic handle part was at least sixteen inches to the rubber part. Melisa closed her eyes and nodded knowingly. Edgar loosened the tape but left it stuck. With time she would be able to free her hands. He walked toward the door, looking back over his shoulder. Melisa began to work the tape off. She hurried at this, thinking maybe she could get out a scream before the door slammed shut. That may result in severe pain in her backside, but it gave her the one thing she longed for—hope.

After Edgar walked to the doorway at a brisk pace, he felt his left leg get even weaker than it had been in the Home Depot parking lot. His left arm felt heavier and more numb. Almost asleep. It stopped responding to him swinging it. The room began spinning as well. Before he knew what was happening, he was on the floor. He could not speak. He could not move. He was practically paralyzed. His thoughts were still his own, and those thoughts were of pure terror. He had loosened her tape! He could hear her working it.

CHAPTER SEVEN

LIKE I SAID BEFORE, a hospitalist physician is like the maître d'
of a fast-food restaurant. Not sure those two things are related, but
essentially I want you in the hospital and greeted warmly. I want you
fed and happy. And then I want you out. Quickly. I do not really
want you out. Medicare does. Medicare invented my job, more or
less. The powers that be had decided in the early 2000s that the old-
school internists who had a waiting room full of patients were
spending too little time at the hospital trying to get their hospitalized patients discharged. They were spending far too much time in
the car between sites or walking to and from the hospital. This atro-
cious behavior was costing millions and millions in excess health care
dollars. So, in the late 1990s, Medicare, or CMS as it is known in
health care circles, stepped in. The upside is that I'm now in the
hospital 24-7. Always. There. The downside is that I do not know
you and never will know you, my patient, as well as your primary
care doctor does. You have known him or her for twenty years. You
have known me for five minutes. And in that five minutes, I'm going
to tell you what's best for you. Then I am going to make sure that
you are ambulating, voiding, stooling, eating, and drinking without

difficulty. Then I am going to kick you out. Whether you really feel better or not. The faster and more efficiently I do this, the happier the hospital is, the more money the billing department will clear, and the better the machine keeps a rollin'. If you remain hospitalized for more than 3.2 days for a routine diagnosis, such as pneumonia, dehydration, congestive heart failure, or COPD, then the hospital actually loses money on your care and administration sends me a nasty email stating that my length-of-stay average is too long and I need to work on that. There is no room for me to retort. "Mrs. Smith wasn't ready to go home. She still felt poorly." Admin does not care. "Get her out, it's been two days."

If there is a bad outcome—such as Mrs. Smith got home and had a heart attack and her husband watched her die on the kitchen floor while waiting for EMS to arrive—well, it was the fault of the incompetent hospitalist physician who sent her home too early. Not the warm and nurturing hospital that hated to see her go.

So, hubby calls whichever billboard ambulance-chasing lawyer had the most recent TV commercial on while he was catching up on old *Magnum, P.I.* episodes. I get sued. Get it? This is how modern hospital medicine has evolved. I've spent fourteen years trying to fly below the radar screen. Not kicking people out too quickly but trying to keep admin happy. As a hospitalist physician, you never want to be the boss. The director, the chief, or the department chair. Your ass will be the first to be fired when things do not go well. The scapegoat. You see, hospital medicine, or internal medicine, does not make money. It costs the hospital and the country money to run. Elective surgeries, plastics, orthopedics, bariatrics. These are the cash cows. My main job is to try to stop the money hemorrhage that internal medicine creates. One uninsured coma patient can keep us in the red for decades. We don't want him in our ICU. So, we push the family to make him a Do Not Resuscitate and withdraw care. Then everyone wins. Except the poor bastard's family who now has to live with their guilt.

This was my life. It used to be set up by a code: husband, father, physician. That order. But when the first one fell apart and my wife left me for SoCal, taking my family with her, it became just physician. I tried to date a little, though I refused to sign up for any online dating. I would just meet women here or there. I refused to date anyone at work. Shitting where you eat is the surest way to get fired in this business. You hear stories of the "call room quickie." You saw this frequently on *Grey's Anatomy*. But it's a bit of an urban legend. However, I will say that my oldest child was conceived in the call room. Not in a romantic tryst type of way but because Shannon was ovulating at the time and I could not get off work as usual. So she visited me at the hospital.

I was at work.

I was at work . . . all the time.

I was at work when my father died. I could not get anyone to cover my shift.

The husband, father, physician credo was changed. To just physician. I had some hobbies, I loved the mountains, but I basically worked all the time.

I was thinking about this as I sat in scrubs in room 438 listening to a thirty-something tell me about her fibromyalgia pain. As an aside, do not ever, *ever* let your primary care or any other physician diagnose you with fibromyalgia. As far as internists and family docs are concerned, it is a made-up diagnosis. It means you cannot cope with life and you are looking for something to blame all of your shit on. We will immediately label you as non-credible, and as a result any real symptom you have will be overlooked.

She had belly pain. Alternating bouts of crampy diarrhea and constipation. No blood in the stool. Could this be inflammatory bowel disease? Crohn's or ulcerative colitis? Yes, it could be. These are real diagnoses, by the way; I would not wish them on my worst enemy. Painful, crippling, lifelong pain-in-the-ass diagnoses. But this was not that. This was irritable bowel syndrome. The ER doc knew this. He was tired of listening to the patient complain for her third straight visit . . . so he sent her to me. Nice fucking guy. It was difficult to remain objective in these cases, but we try anyway. It boiled down to me prescribing a medication called dicyclomine, which really did not work, but it may have had some type of placebo effect in this situation. I talked her through the plan and explained that if this medication did not help, I would be calling the gastroenterologist for a consult. Fibromyalgia and IBS are largely anxiety-based disorders. Not much can be done medically. If I did consult the GI doc, I would be on her shit list as well. So to speak.

CHAPTER EIGHT

MELISA RACKED her brain trying to think of something to do. Some plan of action. Edgar was lying there on the floor, she was free of her restraints, and of course she knew that she should run. But if she did, he may be found and rescued, and he may make up some kind of story that seemed to justify why Melisa was there in the first place. As much of a sadistic monster as he was, he kept the house and even the basement relatively clean. With a good lawyer, he may be able to explain away some of this and he may go free. No one had been looking for Melisa as far as she knew. If Edgar was released, Melisa knew she could never be free. She needed to think. If he died right there, she may be blamed for it. He would not be prosecuted obviously. It could get messy. Her word against his. There was not much proof that she had been his prisoner for all these years. Should she call the police or EMS? Melisa crouched over Edgar, the limp body of her "Daddy." He saw her: he was blinking and staring blankly, the disgusting pig that he was, as if she should be helping him.

A plan started to formulate in her mind. One that would free her of this life and him and maybe even get her some revenge in the process. She was able to pull him to the foot of the stairs but not up them obviously. She straightened up anything that looked suspicious or criminal, like the torn-up duct tape, the chair. The bucket she used for her waste. She left him there and climbed the stairs to the kitchen. He seemed quite incapacitated still. She found the telephone on the wall and dialed 9-1-1.

"Nine one one, operator," the voice said. "What is your emergency?"

"I need help," Melisa said, calmly. "There is something wrong with my grandpa. I think maybe he's had a stroke. He's not moving."

"What is your address? We'll send an ambulance right away."

Melisa realized that she did not know where she was, where she had been held all this time. Not even the town or state. She panicked. She scanned the kitchen counter. There was an envelope from Xcel. It looked like a bill. "We are at 1712 South Holly Street. In Denver. Please hurry." Melisa hung up the phone and sat on the top of the basement stairs watching Edgar. He was out now, but breathing; she could see his chest rise and fall. If he woke or rose, she would bolt. Fast. If he stayed still, she would wait for the paramedics. She looked around the kitchen and the living room from where she sat. It was a nice little house. It looked like a grandpa house. *How had this seemingly normal and sweet man turned into such an evil monster?* she thought. The hard, cold stairs were making her hurt, down there. All the raping, both by him and by objects he had used. Particularly the plunger handle. She hated that one so much. It was still in the basement. Did she have time for a little payback now? Before the EMTs arrived? No. Best not to. Not yet. Her time would come.

Melisa walked to the guest bathroom and looked in the mirror. She had not seen herself in years. She was gaunt and pale. What would be the reason for this if they asked why? She could say she'd been sick. Yeah, the flu. She was feeling better and had been headed out for a walk when she found Grandpa Edgar on the floor of the basement. She saw him from the top of the stairs.

The ambulance siren was getting closer. They would be here any minute. She needed to add some dramatics. She began to cry as she sat on the floor and wept above her impaired assailant. The man who had been raping her and holding her against her will for what she guessed was the last three years. Maybe more.

CHAPTER NINE

FIVE YEARS earlier in San Luis, Colorado, near the New Mexico border

Mama had told Melisa to go play outside. Mama usually told her to do that when the boyfriend came home drunk again. Her own father had left them when Melisa was just a small girl. She had a baby sister, too, Alma, who Mama always called Almita, her little soul. Alma was very sick much of the time. She had the croup. Sometimes Mama would take her to the doctor in Fort Carson or Alamosa, but they never helped much. Alma died when she was two. Melisa's father could not handle the pain, and he left San Luis for Santa Fe or Albuquerque. Melisa could not remember which. He said he would find a better job and make some money and send for them. But he never did. After a few years, Melisa and Mama never heard from him anymore. So Mama found a new boyfriend. He was a bad man named Ricardo, and he did bad things to Mama and tried to do bad things to Melisa too. She would bite him and kick him, though. Then he would curse at her and tell her that one day she would come crawling to him begging for it. *Never*, thought Melisa. Melisa was only ten or eleven years old, but she knew she had to get out of there. If Mama was not going to come with her, she would have to leave on her own. They did not have a car anymore anyway. Her father had taken it. Ricardo had one, but Melisa was too little to drive it. Ricardo was usually drunk on beer when he drove, so the car was always damaged from him crashing into something.

Today, when Mama told Melisa to play outside, she had a plan. She had packed a small canvas bag with her clothes, a small hairbrush, and her doll, Lucy. She was going to walk the three miles to the nearest filling station, a Sinclair station, and wait. A truck would stop there sometime during the day to fill its tank. Melisa had seen this before. Truckers making their way between Taos and Colorado Springs often stopped at the Sinclair to fill their tanks. When the driver went inside, Melisa would hide in the truck and go wherever it went. If she was lucky, it would go to Colorado Springs, and she could get out and find a new family. Maybe even her father. If it went far enough south to Santa Fe.

Melisa felt sorry that now Mama was going to have lost both her daughters. If she could find her father or a new family, maybe they could go back and get her away from Ricardo and his beer breath. Melisa made it to the Sinclair by sundown. A few trucks were filling up then. She saw from the road that one man was heading into the store; he'd come out of a blue truck with red writing on the side. It said ENGLAND TRUCKING or something like that. It was hard to make out because it was in some kind of fancy English writing. Melisa had always been very good in her schoolwork. She loved reading and writing. Math and social studies too. Her class was small. It was summertime, though. Maybe by the time school started again, she could go to a new school in a new town. Far from Ricardo.

The passenger door to the blue truck was unlocked, so Melisa climbed in. It smelled like cigarette smoke and onions. It was a mess. Food wrappers everywhere, ashes. Empty coffee cups. There were a few photographs of children and a family on the dashboard. The trucker's grandchildren maybe? Maybe he was a nice man. Very few of them were. Most of them were mean, or selfish, or rude, or they left you. Melisa hated rude behavior in men. Her husband would be nice. She decided a long time ago.

The trucker came out of the store as Melisa peered through the dirty side door. She and her canvas bag huddled under some towels and a blanket the man had back there. It smelled like pee. But she fit completely under it in the cab behind the passenger seat. Within a minute or two, the man had placed his fresh coffee cup in its holder between the seats, and he pulled the rig out. They were off. It was noisy in there as he shifted and clutched. That was good; he may not hear her.

The road was bumpy and windy; he had to slow down to make some turns and as he climbed through the San Juan Mountains of southeast Colorado. At some point Melisa fell asleep. She wasn't sure how long she was out, but the truck was stopped as she awoke. It was dark and colder outside. *Lucky it's summer*, she thought. She slowly peeked out from under the blanket. The trucker man was gone. There were other trucks next to his. He was back at his home base, she figured. But where? She quietly peeled herself out of the back of the cab and opened the passenger door. No one was there. It was a parking lot. A factory or something, she guessed. As she climbed down the metal stairs from the blue truck, she saw a few men by the doorway of the building. They did not see her. She ran toward the street. It was a quiet one, but she could hear traffic in the distance. She slowed to a walk and headed toward the busy street. She could now see tall buildings, white and gray bricks. There was a big gray building with a gold rounded top a few blocks away. She saw a big green park in front of it. This was not Santa Fe. She had been there once. It didn't look like this. This looked like Washington, DC, a place she had read about in her social studies class with Ms. Salazar. As Melisa walked toward the gold-topped building, she had to cross a busy street. The green sign by the traffic light read Colfax Avenue. As she stepped into the street on the WALK signal, she heard a siren wail and saw flashing lights. She froze where she stood in the street.

CHAPTER TEN

"HOW LONG HAS he been this way?" the paramedic asked Melisa as she now stood over Edgar's limp body.

"I . . . I dunno." Melisa played along. "I was just back from a walk." She realized that she was changing her story but thought it might be understandable coming from a young, frightened girl. "I had been gone maybe an hour or so. I just went to the store." Damn. She had no grocery bags or items if they asked. "He . . . he was just like th-that. When I got home." Playing her part. The scared grand-daughter. Melisa wanted Edgar to survive. She wanted him to be lucid when he realized that she was now in control. That she held his fate in her hands. That time was not now. He wasn't fully aware that his world—the sick, twisted world he had controlled—was ending. She needed him to swing in the breeze. Not knowing if he was going to prison or worse. If there was worse. Melisa did not have all the details worked out yet. She needed more time. She needed him to be cared for in a hospital while she figured it out. Calculated. Melisa had not seen much TV in her lifetime. But she knew that bad things happened to men like him when they went to prison. Things like the things he did to her . . . for many years.

"When did you last see him well?" the second paramedic, this one a woman, asked her.

"Um, I didn't see him this morning. I had left before he woke up. But I saw him last night before bed and he seemed fine then," Melisa explained, her eyes wide open in shock.

This was a typical morning call for the paramedics, the EMTs. The patient was last seen well many hours ago, and as a result there would be little that could be done for him. The guidelines for administering clot-busting, life-saving, or brain-saving medicine were very strict, and if given outside of the specific rules, it could have a disastrous outcome. Such breaches of protocol were all but indefensible on a witness stand. Many an ER physician knows this well.

So it seemed in this case. The EMTs would not have to risk driving on the curb or over any Priuses to get this poor bastard to the ER door. The pair knew that the ER doctor would see the patient quickly. Briefly. The neurologist would do a stroke protocol consult. Then the two physicians would meet at some point and decide that this patient "met exclusion criteria" and would not be administered tPA (Alteplase) in either intravenous or intra-arterial form. He simply arrived too long after his symptoms began. Instead, he would get an aspirin shoved up his ass and some overworked hospitalist would admit him to what was called a neuro-tele unit. This is where all those not lucky enough not to have gotten to the hospital in time ended up.

The paramedics loaded this flaccid man onto a stretcher and then into their rig. The young woman climbed in with them. The female EMT noticed that she still seemed to be wearing pajamas or maybe sweats. They looked dirty. She did not look like someone who had just been to the store. Anyway. Her look was glazed over as well. Concern? Fear? It certainly wasn't obvious.

———

I was finishing my rounds on the med-surg unit when my pager went off. I glanced at the clock on the wall: 12:01 p.m. My call started at noon. Clearly, those eager ER docs were wasting no time getting me going with new admits. This is exactly why I always started making rounds at the hospital early. Usually by six a.m. Because this always happens. Murphy's law. My best friend growing up was named Murphy. Brian Murphy. His dad was a doctor. A gastroenterologist. The family home had a Murphy's law poster hanging on the wall of the basement stairwell. "Whatever can go wrong, will."

I picked up the phone at the nurses' station where I had been finishing my notes and punched in 2455, the emergency department extension.

"ER," the unit clerk mumbled, as she always did when she answered the phone.

"Hey, it's Schwartz. I was promptly paged," I said with my usual hint of sarcasm.

"Yeah. It's Ziller. He wants to talk to you." She put the phone down without hitting the hold button. I was partially relieved. I hated hold music, especially in hospitals. These days it is more advertising, though. I know our breast imaging center is state-of-the-art. I don't need it beaten into my skull.

"Ziller," my buddy Andy said into the phone once he picked it up. Always in his calm, Duke-educated voice.

"Andy, it's Mike Schwartz. Whatcha got for me?"

"Umm . . . for you . . . sixty-ish white male. Name escapes me. Probable stroke. Ischemic. Total left-sided hemiplegia. Paralysis of his left side. Upper and lower extremities. Aphasic. Facial droop on the right. CTA head and neck shows massive right-sided M2 occlusion with MCA distribution. Whole left parietal ischemia and thalamic involvement as well."

(Translation: elderly white gentleman has suffered a blood clot or blood vessel blockage to a medium-sized artery that supplies blood to the area of the brain that provides motor function to the left side of the body, including the arm and leg as well as the areas that control speech as well as the "switch station" of the brain that tells the extremities precisely how to move.)

"When?" I asked, simply. Always the main concern in a stroke like this.

"Don't know time of onset, unfortunately," my friend said. "Granddaughter, who lives with him or was maybe visiting him, went out for a walk this morning, came home to find him like that on the floor of the basement. She had not seen him since bedtime the night before. Approximately eighteen hours ago now." Ziller glanced at the paramedic notes scribbled on the front of the ER chart.

"What did neuro say? And which doc was it?" I would need to document the neurologist's name in my note stating that the ER doc had spoken with him and had completed a formal consult. All stroke alerts had this documentation standard. Big money in stroke lawsuits. Missing one detail of the patient's physical exam or not documenting the neurologist's consult or not acting in proper time-line could mean your ass and your license.

"Jensen. He's still here talking to the granddaughter. He says no IV or IA tPA given the extent of the damage and obviously since we missed the window," Andy said. I figured as much. (Translation: since the patient had arrived at the hospital past four hours after the time of onset of his symptoms, he was excluded from the possibility of having blood-clot busting medicine given to him in his IV site or in a fancy room by a neuroradiologist directly into the artery in his brain that was blocked.)

"Poor guy. All right. I'll be there in five. Let's get a neuro step-down unit bed for him, please. Inpatient status." (Translation: not the ICU but the next highest level of care bed we offer.) I gave the kindly ER doc my preference of unit for this new patient. But my orders were rarely carried out when it came to geography. I was the Rodney Dangerfield of hospital medicine. No respect. The house supervisor would review the case presentation and decide if she felt that my unit preference for my patient was something her over-worked nursing staff could accommodate in that unit or if he should be placed somewhere less busy. The difference between a monitored bed or an unmonitored one. I stopped dying on that particular hill years ago. It was her house. Her nurses. If she felt something else would work better, so be it. I was not an egomaniacal doc. Many docs are, though.

I finished up a few orders in some med-surg unit charts and made my way down the staircase to the ER. I stopped to use the restroom off the hospital lobby. Coffee, water, and LaCroix all day combined with my infant-sized bladder led to very frequent bathroom visits throughout the day.

After my quick pit stop, a swipe of my ID badge got me access through the backdoor of the ED. This was the door closest to the behavioral health unit of the ER. Lots of interesting characters in there. Lots of intense psychiatric pathology. Last week a girl all of twenty-two years old was tweaking on meth laced with something making her very paranoid. She plucked out both her eyeballs, throwing the left one on the floor. The right one was still dangling from the optic nerve in front of her right cheekbone. An ophthalmologist and a trauma surgeon worked on her for over eight hours in the OR but were not able to save the right eye. So she is blind now, obviously. To make matters worse, while she was screaming in the ER about her headache, she actually suffered a stroke as well. Now she is paralyzed on the left side of her body. Her family is suing the ER doctor and physician assistant (PA) who were caring for her. Suing the hospital too. For negligence. Both providers had been unable to get near her, however, for an examination as she was kicking and screaming. In just that instant, she was able to grab a spoon off a nearby tray and pop out the two orbits. When she did the deed, the doc had run to order 20 mg of Geodon, an antipsychotic med, to be injected into her arm. The doc never had any chance to help her, but the family and their attorney, of course, served him with papers anyway, citing his lack of proper care. "Delay in diagnosis" was a big money maker for these vultures. Lawyers, not the family, of course. I do not believe there was a doctor on this earth who could have helped her in time. But the family will try to get some cash from the hospital to help with the bills that will accumulate while they are caring for this girl for the next sixty years or so.

It is a fucked, fucked, fucked-up world.

———

I knocked on the door of Treatment Room 2, the room where I would find my new stroke patient. I glanced at him. Older white guy. Balding. A bit overweight. Looked like a lot of patients. One's health really starts to decline once you hit your sixties if you have not done anything to counter it. He had faded tattoos on his forearms. One was an anchor. Like Popeye. This was a former Navy man. His vital signs flashed on the monitor. His BP was a little high at 170/90 mmHg, but that is to be expected when one has had a stroke. The man was out of it. Sleeping. Probably had a long morning.

A girl of maybe nineteen or twenty sat on the orange plastic chair near the bed. She also seemed a tad out of it. A little disheveled too, I might add. "Hi," I said loudly. "I'm Dr. Schwartz. I'm one of the admitting doctors. I'm called a hospitalist. Did the ER doctor tell you we would be admitting your . . ."

"Grandpa," the girl piped up, without looking up at me or him. "I'm Melisa. Yes, he did tell me that, or the nurse."

"Oh, okay. Well, it seems he's had a stroke. A large one. It's what we call an ischemic stroke. So, no hemorrhage or bleeding into the brain. But a large area over part of his brain"—I circled my hand around the right parietal/temporal part of his head—"has suffered a lack of blood flow and therefore oxygen, and that's what caused his collapse." I peeked at the EMS report on the chart on the counter near the sink. "You found him down, right?"

"Yes," Melisa, the girl, said. Again not glancing at me nor him.

"I apologize for the redundancy. I know that you've been asked these questions probably ten times by now," I added in a lower voice. When you deal in geriatrics, you tend to raise your voice, even when your patients can hear you. I have been told even by elderly patients not to shout at them. Usually it saves time, however.

"It's okay," Melisa said. "I don't mind."

"Good. Thank you. Are there any other members of the family we can expect to come to the hospital?" I inquired.

"No. Just us. Just him and me. For years." Melisa gazed out the door of Treatment Room 2 into the chaos of the busy ED.

CHAPTER ELEVEN

THE SCREECH of the siren and the bright blue light caused Melisa to jump back quickly off busy Colfax Avenue. The police car pulled up and stopped, blocking her from stepping off the curb again. The driver clearly was not bothered that the street was busy with cars. No one would dare honk. They just went around the cop like he was a homeless man you sidestep rather than drop a quarter in his cup.

A female officer jumped out of the passenger side. "What do you think you're doing, young lady? You are gonna get run over crossing here. You gotta use the crosswalk." She pointed up the block toward the gold-topped building.

"Lo siento. No entiendo, señora," Melisa said. She turned the way the officer pointed but felt her hand on her shoulder.

"Where's your parents? You all by yourself out here?" The officer looked a bit more stern now.

"No hablo inglés," Melisa said, trying to formulate a plan to buy herself time. If she said she had run away, they would try to send her back to San Luis. If she played dumb, maybe she could figure out a way to stay here.

The officer yelled something to her partner behind the wheel. Then she grabbed the walkie-talkie thing attached to her shoulder and said something into it about a minor alone she was bringing into central processing. Then she said, "Over," and clicked it off.

"All right, little lady. Let's get in the car." And with that she opened the rear door for Melisa to get in. Not the plan she had hoped for. But at least she was away from Ricardo and his beer breath.

———

Melisa pretended not to understand English for about another day and a half. The police had given her to a Spanish-speaking woman who had a small office in the building next to the police station. She said her name was Lydia and she was a social worker. Since Melisa had no ID and was not answering any questions, Lydia said they were going to try to find foster care for her. They had nowhere to send her, and she would need shelter and food and schooling. Lydia assumed that whatever happened to this poor girl was so horrendous that she either did not remember or did not want to remember. Trauma of some kind. Lydia would arrange some counseling for her, of course, but in the meantime see if there was a Spanish-speaking family with whom she could stay.

Lydia made a cursory attempt at a search for relatives. The girl had told her that her name was Melisa Ramos. Lydia had no way to verify this, so that was the name she entered for her search through the Centers for Missing and Exploited Children. Since this was a reasonably large database, it required a few things to be successful. Accurate name and description of the missing child. And an actual report that the individual was missing in the first place. If Melisa's family was illegal, they'd likely not report a child missing. It could create heat for the whole family, and there may be a large group hidden away somewhere. Because of the high rate of failure, Lydia was not going to devote too much time and effort to finding Melisa's family. Lydia would play the odds. If the girl was missing and someone loved her and missed her, then they would come looking for her. That was the best that could be done for now.

Melisa was first placed with a family in Thornton. The social workers and case managers had determined that she was eleven years old. She'd had a brief physical exam with a nurse practitioner who deemed her a healthy preteen. Thornton, Colorado, was a northern suburb of Denver. It had a large Latino population. In addition, lots of drugs and alcohol. But a few kind families had been helpful in taking in foster kids from south of the border. They got a little money from the state for this, but Lydia knew several of the families well and felt that Melisa would at least get a fighting chance at a life if she started out here. These were short-term placements. The families would provide a place to live and to sleep, and access to the local public school. Greeley Elementary was down the block from one such family's home. The Rodriguez family has six of their own children, and they were stretched thin. Emilio was the father, and he worked at one of the ore mills in Commerce City, a real shithole of a town next door. He made $11.50 an hour there, and taking in foster kids had helped Graciela, as his wife added another $160 per week per kid to the mix. She could feed a child on about $25 a week and pocket the rest. Lydia was not thrilled, but it was a start. Once the fee dropped to $130 per week, which it did after four months, Graciela would invent some reason why the kid couldn't stay there anymore.

Since it was now fall, school was starting. Melisa was living with the Rodriguez family in Thornton, Colorado, and was enrolled at Greeley Elementary in the fifth grade. She did remarkably well. She spoke English and Spanish and excelled at math and social studies. She felt safe at school, and none of the kids messed with her like some were messed with from other homes down the block. Melisa had heard stories at school. She missed Mama, of course, but her little mind was always trying to think of ways she could find her one day. In four years, she may learn to drive. Maybe she could get a car. Maybe drive to San Luis and get Mama away from Ricardo.

True to her reputation, Graciela called Lydia after four months. It was now January and very cold. She said that she and Emilio were having trouble paying the bills and she had her other children to think about. She could not keep Melisa anymore. But when there was a new child soon, she would be happy to help. Once the bills were paid.

Lydia picked Melisa up one Saturday and drove her away in a small car with an H on the hood. Right past Melisa's school. She did not even get to say good-bye to her classmates. Lydia said little as she drove. Still, she made small talk about a lovely family in a place called Aurora who had a small room Melisa could stay in. There was a school nearby, but Melisa would have to take a bus to that one. Melisa leaned her head against the cold glass window and tried to hold back her tears.

CHAPTER TWELVE

I GREW up in the suburbs of Denver. My family had moved to Colorado from Chicago when I was very little. Two or three years old. The high school basketball coaching job my father had taken at Kinsey Prep in Denver was apparently much better than the one he'd left behind at New Lyons Academy in Chicago. Something about budget cuts, he would grumble. He didn't care where, he just wanted to coach. So, I grew up on Milwaukee Street in Denver. My parents unable to afford to purchase a home, the house was a rental. An old one at that. I remember my mother always talking about how "charming" it was. I had mentioned earlier my best friend, Brian Murphy, who lived down the street. The one with the poster on the wall about Murphy's Law. It was a great place to live. To grow up. I thought so anyway. I was raised partially as an only child. I wasn't born an only child. I was the younger brother. The four of us made the journey to Denver. My sister was two and a half years older than me. When I was seven, she never made it home from school one day. It was a spring day. Our school was around the corner and four blocks down. It was a Waldorf school. Fourth grade was wrapping up for the year, and my mother had been helping at the end-of-the-year class party. My sister, Jean, wanted to walk home and see our new puppy, Leo. He was a beagle. Jean was obsessed with him. My mother said it was okay for her to walk home as long as she looked both ways when she crossed the three streets: St Paul, Steele, and Milwaukee.

Jean promised she would and then started out at a moderate trot to get home to play with Leo. Basketball season was long over, so my father would be home. My class was still having its party, and Mom would walk me home afterward.

Jean was last seen crossing St. Paul Street, the busiest of the streets that intersected in front of the school. That was it. No one ever reported seeing her again. Alive. The story was that a brown van, a Chevy, came to a stop alongside her. The sliding door opened, and one man grabbed her while the other sped away behind the wheel. Witnesses reported this to the police who had arrived on the scene quickly. A neighbor out watering plants, an elderly woman, was the first. Her description was minimally helpful as she was near-sighted, but once word spread of a missing girl from the neighbor-hood, a manhunt ensued.

There hadn't been an abduction in that part of Denver for thirty years, and the police were eager not to break that streak with a tragedy. They would not get their wish, however. My sister's body was found in Cheesman Park the next morning. Not two miles from our house on Milwaukee Street. A jogger found her. Early in the morning, before sunrise. Jean had been beaten severely. Raped repeatedly and ultimately strangled to death. The medical examiner explained to my parents that since the first two events happened before the third, she likely would have been in pain when she died. My mother had asked if she suffered. I remember thinking, *Why could you not have lied to her?* I would later learn that the medical examiner's testimony would be very important in court and that all of her statements needed to be accurate and truthful throughout the investigation so that the court record would be pristine. Not so great for Jean's family, it seemed. They caught one of the men after some months, and he was tried in court. They were druggies. Drifters. The perp said they were so high they barely remembered the girl but knew they had to get rid of her. The other died in a heroin overdose, the first said. They had sold the van for drug money. This guy got caught when he tried to purse snatch on Clayton Street in the Cherry Creek section of town.

My parents attended his trial as well as the sentencing. The judge allowed them both the opportunity to speak in court on my sister's behalf. Neither could bring themselves to do so. The assailant was allowed to speak at his sentencing. He gave a weak apology for his crimes and said that my sister was the first and only child this pair had ever kidnapped. He blamed the drugs and heavy metal music for his behavior. This transient, drug-riddled man was given two life sentences to be served consecutively at Colorado's "Supermax" facility ADX in Florence, Colorado. He was thirty-eight years old. No chance of parole. Later, our grief counselor explained that Jean was almost certainly not the only victim of these two men and they likely had a pattern of predatory behavior with multiple victims in multiple states. We could take solace in the fact that Jean was the hero that got them caught. Ended their terror. A strange way to look at it, but it gave my parents some peace nonetheless.

"Beware the brown van" was a mantra that spread throughout the neighborhoods of Denver. "Watch out! The brown van!" the kids would scream, almost playfully, after that. An urban legend like the boogeyman. Stories circulated through the streets and elementary schools. I do not think I ever slept through the night after that. I would stay up late and read. Practically all night long. Any book that I could get my hands on. Adventure stories, crime stories, science fiction were my favorites, though. Then, when I was in junior high school, I would study practically all night. This habit continued through high school and into college. It is probably why I got into medical school.

None of this brought her back, of course. It wasn't the fact that she was gone that bothered me so much and kept me awake all those nights. It's that it was so senseless. So random, so violent, and so meaningless. That was what bothered me so much, what still bothers me. It's difficult to imagine someone so evil. To destroy a life, to rape a child. Prison, and the horrors that go with it, just do not seem like enough justice. When I was finishing medical school, I seriously considered going into neuropsychiatry. I thought maybe if I could get inside the psyche of these deranged monsters, I could get some closure based on insight into the pathology that caused it. After a while, however, I realized that these two men were more likely just born pure evil and needed to be put down. I specialized in internal medicine instead. I have not slept well since I was eight years old.

CHAPTER THIRTEEN

I BEGAN my examination of Edgar Shivers—the sixty-eight-year-old man who had apparently suffered a stroke sometime in the last twelve to eighteen hours. He had a helpless gaze on his face as he looked off to the right. Gaze preference, we call this. He was weakened and clearly scared. A common presentation in a big, busy ER.

My examination concluded much as the neurologist's and ER doctor's had: dense left-sided hemiplegia with expressive aphasia and right-sided facial droop. Classic MCA distribution stroke. He could not move the left side of his body, couldn't speak, and had facial weakness, which would likely also accompany swallowing difficulty, and therefore eating and drinking would be impeded. These MCA (middle cerebral artery) strokes could be quite devastating and required a great deal of rehabilitation to overcome symptomatically. First, the patient would need more work up, though, more tests. More evaluation to determine where the stroke came from. What caused it? Ischemic strokes like this one came in two varieties: embolic and thrombotic. The first refers to a blood clot that travels to the brain, typically from the heart and often associated with a condition called atrial fibrillation. The second type occurs due to a blockage in the arterial wall itself within the brain that has been developing over time, often from a history of high blood pressure, diabetes, high cholesterol, and smoking cigarettes.

Mr. Shivers probably had the latter and a combination of the risk factors listed. Now it was my job to try to figure out to which of these factors he had been predisposed to. The most important risk factor, and the one we can do the least about, is family history, however.

"Melisa, is it okay if I call you Melisa?"

She turned her eyes to me, blinked, and said, "Sure, I guess."

I continued, "Do you know if there's a family history of these types of events, strokes? Your grandpa's parents, for instance? Perhaps a brother or sister of his?"

"Um . . . I dunno. I never met anyone in his family. He didn't talk about them," Melisa said quickly, rubbing her eye as if a tear was there.

"Oh, okay," I offered, to ease her mind. "No worries. Well, let me step out for a minute and get some orders in the chart so we can get your grandfather a bed upstairs. I'll see you up in his room, okay?" I smiled at her and left the exam room thinking that it was odd that she said "*his* family."

———

Melisa was terrified. She did not want this doctor or anyone to think that she had anything to do with Edgar getting sick. She had been with him so long, she did not even remember her last foster family very well, let alone Mama down in San Luis. How long had it been since she'd seen anyone who cared about her? Two years? Three?

A nurse came in to unhook the IV tubing and the heart monitor leads from Edgar so that he could be transported upstairs to his room. She started bundling up the wires and pumps and placed them next to Edgar on the gurney. "Time to head up," she said. "Telemetry-neuro unit. Fourth floor." None of these words meant anything to Melisa. She simply sat on the edge of her plastic chair. Melisa began thinking about the foster family she had been living with when Edgar took her. They were not the most loving people.

Her foster parents fought a lot. The man drank. He stayed out late, sometimes all night. Much like Ricardo had done. When her foster dad, Geoff, did come home, her foster mom, Christie, would scream at him and throw things. Cursing. Horrible words she would say. Melisa would be home sometimes when they fought. She would run outside, even if it was cold. She would walk around the block. Around the neighborhood. Sometimes she brought her secondhand Snoopy suitcase with her. Melisa could hear Geoff and Christie screaming at each other all the way down the street. She was confident the people in the other houses could hear them too. It was certainly no secret that the family on South Locust Street had major issues. It wasn't exactly an affluent part of Denver anyway. Melisa would be gone for hours at a time. Walking. Dreaming. Thinking about Mama in San Luis. That is what she was doing the day the yellow Subaru Baja pulled over to her.

"Are you coming with us, hon?" Melisa looked up at the nurse and the transport tech. The nurse gestured toward the curtain opening and door of Treatment Room 2.

"Um, yes. Thank you." Melisa gathered herself and followed the nurse down the busy, noisy hallway of the emergency department. In one room she saw a man getting some kind of tube shoved down his nose. He was gagging. In another room a woman was standing dazed, urinating on the floor. In still another, a doctor was hovering over a teenage boy, about Melisa's age, trying to get some sort of wire into his neck. It was disturbing. Melisa just followed the nurse and the tech. And her "grandpa," Edgar. The man who kept her chained in his basement since that day he pulled over in his Baja. He had been putting himself inside her since then. Melisa could not get her mind past that. He was lying now on the gurney as the tech pushed him down the hallway. Why did Melisa stay silent? Why did she not run? Shout, scream, hit? There was only one thing she kept coming back to.

More than any of those things, she wanted to watch him die.

CHAPTER FOURTEEN

I WAS DOWN in radiology looking at the MRI results of Mr. Shivers's brain. "Devastating," Dr. Sarti said. My radiologist buddy was peering at the T2-FLAIR images of the sixty-eight-year-old. "His entire right parietal-temporal brain region is toast. This guy will never talk, walk, or feed himself again." I thought of the implications of this. "Has he got any family?" Sarti asked me.

"Um, yes, there is a teenage girl in the room with him," I answered.

"Well, she won't be able to handle this. Get physical therapy and occupational therapy to see him, but he's going to be total care. Nursing home from now on. At age sixty-eight. Sucks."

"Thanks, Marc, as always." I jotted down a few notes on my clipboard and trudged out of the radiology department thinking that this upcoming conversation was going to require more coffee. The doc's lounge on the first floor had a few Keurig cups left but only whole milk left in the fridge. Gross. I thought, *Black it is today*. I sipped the cup slowly as I climbed the four flights of stairs to the neuro-tele unit where Mr. Shivers and his granddaughter were. Waiting. For me. For news. I still try to take the stairs as much as I could. Hospital medicine is a young man's game. I wasn't that anymore. So the only way to stay competitive was to stay fit. I hoofed it every chance I got. And I got a lot of chances. All code blues and rapid response alerts (which were usually called prior to code blues for patient distress) required stairs and hallways anyway. Stairs were the lifeblood of hospital transit. At least to the docs, nurses, and techs who ran the place.

When I reached the fourth floor, I set my clipboard and coffee cup on the countertop, then popped a breath mint into my mouth. Coffee breath wouldn't do in this case. I knocked gently on the door of room 402 as I pushed the handle open slightly.

"Mr. Shivers, Melisa?" I said quietly. "It's Dr. Schwartz. May I come in?"

————

Melisa had nodded off slightly as *The Golden Girls* laugh track was audible on the dated, wall-mounted TV in room 402. She had noted that all the channels on the TV were geared toward older people. She herself had not seen a TV channel in years, but she knew *The Golden Girls*, *Andy Griffith*, and the Hallmark Channel. These three were meant to give senior-aged patients a sense of familiarity. Plus, these channels were probably cheaper than HBO for the hospital to provide.

She heard the knock and the young-looking doctor open the door. Melisa jilted upright. She wiped her face in case of any drool.

"Hi, Dr. Schwartz." His face lacked any clear expression. He pulled up one of the two schoolroom-type chairs from the wall toward the bed. Melisa was sitting in the recliner near the window.

"I'm afraid the news is not good," Dr. Schwartz began. "The area of his brain responsible for movement of his left side as well as speech, swallowing, and even some cognitive brain function has been badly damaged." The doctor stood up and sketched a crude picture on the dry erase board under the TV. The board listed the date, the tests that were planned, and the nursing assignment for the shift. Dr. Schwartz began shading in a large area of a circular structure, which Melisa surmised was the brain itself. Edgar just lay there blinking every three to four seconds. "Your grandfather will need intensive physical, occupational, speech, and cognitive therapy for several months. If not longer. And even then, his prognosis is quite poor." Melisa absorbed this news.

"Where will all of this therapy be?" she asked slowly.

The doctor looked at both their faces and then said, "At first, in what we call an acute rehab center. Inpatient type, he would stay there for weeks. Three hours a day of exercises. It is intense. Medicare will only pay for three weeks of this type of care, however. Your grandfather will need full-time care after that, probably permanently. In a nursing home. For the rest of his life. Which will now be much shorter than it otherwise may have been." Dr. Schwartz then gave Melisa a look that she interpreted as, *He is pretty much fucked.*

"And what will happen to me?" Melisa asked, and she almost broke down.

Dr. Schwartz moved his chair slightly closer to her, leaned forward, and said, "Well, you'll be in charge of his affairs. His estate. His house, I guess. It's not really my area, but I'm happy to have Jaime, my case manager, come in next and discuss with you all of the options. It is a great deal of paperwork, faxing. I'm not going to lie to you, it's not pleasant." Dr. Schwartz paused. "You seem like a strong person. You can handle this."

You have no idea, Melisa thought to herself.

"We will do everything we can to help you." As he said this, Dr. Schwartz was remembering two things: the first was that he was still the maître d' and he needed a discharge plan for this man with a severe stroke. The second thought was about how everyone had been so "helpful" when his sister had been taken, raped, and murdered. Everyone loves to "help." It was horseshit. His brand was no different.

Melisa stood from the recliner and turned toward the window. A moment passed, then she turned and moved back to the head of the bed. She leaned over Edgar Shivers's face so that it was only about two inches from her own. She stared at him.

"Doctor, what is that term that means whatever is between yourself and your patient remains confidential? Hippo something?"

"HIPAA," Michael corrected. "Health Insurance Portability and Accountability Act."

"Yes. That's it," Melisa said, not moving from her spot, instead still hovering above Edgar. "If I tell you something about this patient of yours, you can't report it, right?"

"Well, yes, Melisa, that's correct." Michael tensed. "Not without his permission."

Melisa kept her bent posture but turned her head to look at Dr. Schwartz. "He is not my grandfather. Until two or three years ago, I had never met him before. He's my abductor. We are not related."

Michael sat down again.

Melisa continued, "My abductor. My captor. My rapist. My sodomizer. My assaulter. And my nightmare. And now, as I see it"—she paused—"I am his."

CHAPTER FIFTEEN

I WAS FLABBERGASTED. Stunned by what I had just heard. I
was glad at that moment that I was sitting. Shocked. Appalled. In
utter disbelief. I had a hand raised off my knee going to cover my
mouth as if in theater watching a horror movie, then realized that
was an unprofessional look, so I stopped and sat upright.

"Why didn't you call the police? This morning? Why did you call
the paramedics?" I somehow managed to ask her.

Melisa crossed her arms and looked at the floor. "I've been
wondering that all day. I can't explain it very well. I've been trapped
with this . . . man for . . . three years? Maybe more. When he fell
this morning, I was in shock. I am so used to retaliation for any out-
of-line behavior, my first thought was, *Don't step out of line.* I called
9-1-1 before I'd even thought about it. While I was waiting for the
ambulance, it occurred to me for the first time that I was finally in
control. But I was exhausted. I *am* exhausted. My anger was simmer-
ing, but taking it out on him right then was beyond me.

"I thought, *If I can find out what's wrong, I'll tell someone at the
hospital. If he doesn't die, he'll be arrested.* If he got better, maybe he'd
go free. Or not spend too much time in jail, if any. That's too good
for . . . him. This animal. This monster."

I tried to get my mind around all of this. "I'm so sorry," was all I could muster. "Miss . . . I'm sorry, I don't actually know your real name."

"My name really is Melisa. Melisa Ramos."

"Melisa, we need to get you to the ER. We need to do a full exam and check for any injuries. There may be infections, other signs of physical abuse. May we do that?" I asked hopefully.

"No. I'm sorry, doctor. I have no doubt that there are injuries. I doubt there are STDs. The sadistic piece of shit has not been able to get it up in months. He would beat and rape me usually with a wooden handle. From a toilet plunger," she said with a smirk that was almost a tear. "I would bleed for hours and days. I'm quite sure that I can no longer have children. I would bleed sometimes without any cause. I don't want to know the extent of the damage. Not yet anyway." Melisa uncrossed her arms and leaned on the window, looking out.

"Melisa, we need to notify the police. And hospital administration," I pleaded. "And we need to do it now."

"Absolutely not. Not until I've thought this through. What do you doctors say? Processed it. Then, maybe. And if you go behind my back, I will tell the newspapers, media outlets, anyone who will listen, that you violated my trust. Broke HIPAA laws. It won't matter if it's not true. You'll be finished professionally." She glanced at my ID badge for a long moment. "I don't want to do that, Dr. Schwartz. But I'm a survivor. I'll do whatever it takes to survive."

Not believing I could be more shocked than I had been just a few moments ago, now I was practically floored. This young woman was in some kind of fugue state. Either she was the most cunning, obsessive person in the world, planning moves three, four steps ahead, or more likely, she was in shock. Post traumatized, confused, angered, possibly psychotic, and in need of help. So, I said what doctors say, "What can I do to help?"

As soon as I had said it, I realized that I was, on some level, offering to assist her in her scheme—whatever that was or would be, but I had to start somewhere. Melisa sat down again, facing me. "You keep your evaluation going. Order your tests. Consult with your specialists. While you do that, I will figure out the best next step for me. Now, I need some rest. Can you have someone bring me a cot or something?"

"Um, sure. I suppose I can do that." I looked her in the eyes. "You have to promise me, Melisa, that you won't do anything irrational while I'm gone. Can you do that for me?" I pleaded.

"Of course, Dr. Schwartz. I won't lay a hand on him." She almost smiled, which both comforted and scared the shit out of me. I slowly left the room, closed the door, and headed for the nurses' station. I'm sure I looked white as a sheet because Kelly Richards, the nurse for room 402, Mr. Shivers's room approached me.

"Dr. Schwartz, you feeling okay?" she steadied me.

"What? Yes, I'm sorry, always hard to deliver bad news. The girl in there. With him. Can't be older than seventeen."

"His granddaughter. Yeah. Tough break for her too. Do they need anything?" Kelly asked.

"Yeah, a rollaway bed, please. She said that she would like to get some sleep."

"Wouldn't we all," Kelly retorted, then walked away toward central supply.

———

Fifteen years. Fifteen years in this business and I had thought I had seen everything. Seen it all. What a fool I was. But nothing prepares you for this kind of situation. I knew deep down that Melisa's threat was not real. If I came forward with it, then she denied it, which she would, I would look like a lunatic. Which was worse, a lunatic who violated his patient's confidential medical and social history. I would have a serious asterisk on my record moving forward. Not a good thing for a man trying to support a family from afar. If Melisa truly was the victim of such heinous acts, what was she capable of doing? Did I want to find out?

I awoke that night in my small apartment in a cold sweat. I had been dreaming about the brown van circling my childhood neighborhood. I heard my older sister's screams as she was carried off and locked inside the van. Darkness. Horrors. Realizing that sleep would be impossible to achieve again, I climbed out of bed at two a.m. and sat at my computer. I Googled Melisa Ramos, Denver, Colorado. I found about a hundred entries. No way to sort through them all. I did not even know how to narrow. Nothing jumped off the pages with the words *abducted, kidnapped, victim,* or *missing.* Finding this a dead end, I went for a run. Then I hit the jump rope in the courtyard and killed time until my gym in Glendale would open at 5:00 a.m. for some weights.

After a shower and a cup of coffee, I started to feel better. More clear-headed. I headed for the hospital and made my way to the neuro-tele unit. Room 402.

———

Melisa was able to sleep soundly. Probably for the first time in years. Ironically, her captor slept only a few feet from her. She was no longer afraid. No longer vulnerable. She was now empowered, and she felt that power. She was rubbing her eyes when the short knock of the infamous Dr. Schwartz rang out and the door pushed open.

He entered and stood near her but not too near. His arms were crossed around a clipboard, and he wore no lab coat but a shirt and tie. "Well. How are we doing today?" he asked cautiously.

"We're fine." Melisa got up, walked to the bathroom, began brushing her teeth with the kit the nurse had procured for her.

"Any news of which I should be made aware? Any change in our disposition?" Schwartz asked.

Melisa wiped her mouth as she entered the room. "He's the same. Snored all night. Like pigs do. No, Doctor, no change with the plan. It is the same as it was last night. I stay here with him until I have figured out the best way for me to gain closure on what's been my life for the last three years. I was very insightful once. A good student. I could have been anything. I could have been a doctor like you. I had already come far. He . . . robbed me of that. I have been through hell already. I climbed out of its depths. I need time, Dr. Schwartz." Melisa sat down in the recliner and even managed a smile.

Michael sat too. On the plastic chair. He leaned forward in his professional mode. "Ms. Ramos, Melisa, I get it. More than you know. Life is not black and white. We will keep working on Mr. Shivers and evaluating his progress and prognosis. In the meantime, I've brought this for you." He handed her a business card. "It's a group. It's anonymous. For survivors. Like you. I've referred several patients and family members of patients to them in the past. Not that you're a patient and not that you're a family member of a patient. But I feel the conditions are similar. Would you be willing to meet with them? One time is all that I ask. I suspect that it will help you. I think it will help you gain the closure you seek. Or a pathway to it. Peacefully."

Melisa looked at the card. It was a group that met twice weekly. In the basement of a church near the hospital. On Clermont Street. She thought for a minute.

"Will you go with me?" Melisa asked without taking her eyes off the card.

"Um, sure . . . I guess. It meets tonight. Eight o'clock."

"I'll see you there, Doc." With that, Melisa closed her eyes and leaned back, making the recliner squeak.

CHAPTER SIXTEEN

MELISA WOKE LATER, showered in the bathroom of room 402, and changed her clothes. The charge nurse had managed to find some secondhand ones in the lost and found, likely left behind by deceased patients, Melisa thought. A pair of old jeans and a well-worn Broncos sweatshirt. It still had the logo from the seventies on it. It was faded orange, but it would do. It was baggy enough to conceal the fact that Melisa did not have on a bra. She did not own a bra based on her recent living arrangement. Something she would have to deal with later. She was in the bathroom trying to arrange her hair a bit. It had been years since she was in a social situation. That fact was a bit intimidating. At this point, it mattered little to Melisa. After what she had been through, she could handle most anything, most anyone.

She left the hospital through the main entrance and started walking the five blocks to the church. It was located at Clermont and 7th Streets. On the corner. Melisa found the entrance and the stairs. There was sign at the door welcoming all faiths, creeds, and gender identities. That seemed friendly to her. Hopefully, the people inside would be warm as well. The stairs were just past the doorway and Melisa took them down. The basement was lit by fluorescent lights, many of which were burnt out and the remaining ones made a humming sound indicating they were on their last legs as well. Some even flickered. It looked like something out of the *Fight Club* movie set, a movie she had seen on TV at the foster home before she was taken by Edgar.

There was a coffee pot on a warmer in the corner, and standing by it she saw Dr. Schwartz. He was sipping from a cup and looking at his cell phone. As he fiddled with the phone, scrolling, he walked toward the empty seats and chose one. Melisa walked to the coffee pot and poured herself some coffee into a small Styrofoam cup. There was no milk or creamer, but some sugar packets were strewn about. She tore two open and poured them in. No stirrers. Melisa then took a seat next to Dr. Schwartz. He glanced at her doing so and shuffled in his seat a bit trying to relax. Clearly, she made him nervous. There were about fifteen other "guests" in attendance. Mostly young women, a few men, though. Some other teenagers.

"Welcome," a pleasant-looking lady said with a smile. She had a long braid down her back, rings on several of her fingers, and Birkenstocks with thick wool socks. Faded jeans were tucked into the socks. "I'm Michelle." She looked around the room to make eye contact with all the guests. The chairs had been arranged in a circular pattern so all the patrons could see each other. "There is no need to respond with "Hi, Michelle,'" she said with a wink. "This is not that kind of group. We will get to know each other as part as part of the healing process. We will share and laugh and cry and listen. Through this, we will Take Back . . . and we will grow stronger. We will celebrate in the joy that we are here. We aren't dead. We are victorious. We are . . . survivors. We . . . are survivors," she added with emphasis. "So, thank you. All of you. For coming here tonight. Welcome back to my repeat friends. A special welcome to my new visitors and friends. Welcome," she said again and added a little fist raise. "Please help yourself to coffee and treats. Take a deep breath." Michelle paused. "We are survivors. Of sexual abuse. Physical abuse and emotional abuse. We . . . are . . . survivors." She looked at the group again with an encouraging smile. "Who would like to start?"

"I would." A hand went up two chairs to the left of Michael Schwartz.

"Please," Michelle said warmly. "We are all here for you. Why don't you start with your name?"

The teenage girl, younger than Melisa, shuffled her feet. She bit her lower lip. A small tear fell off her left cheek. The older woman next to her, her mom perhaps, put an arm around the girl and gave a squeeze.

"My therapist said that coming to this group would be a good idea. My name is Brianna. I'm sixteen. I would be a junior at West High School. I don't go to school anymore, though. When I was a freshman, fourteen years old, I was raped. Repeatedly, by my music teacher. My guitar teacher, I guess I meant. I play . . . played guitar. Classical guitar. I was good." Brianna looked around at the faces seated in the chairs. As if for assurance of her statement.

"My teacher said I may go to Juilliard. His name was . . . is David. David Poe."

"Oh, no names, please, Brianna. Except your first name," Michelle interrupted.

"Yes, sorry." Brianna sniffled back some tears. "We wouldn't want to invade the privacy of the perverts, would we?" Brianna said this and sobbed for a moment. "I'm sorry. I'm sorry, Michelle. Sorry, guys," she said to the group. "It's hard for me."

"It's okay, sweetie. It's okay, Brianna. Take your time, we are all here for you," Michelle said again.

Brianna took a deep breath. She continued, "At first, he was very stern, very strict. Any mistake, he would berate me, slap the ruler on the music stand. Sometimes on my hand. I wanted to please him. I wanted to be perfect." Brianna looked at her mother. "I wanted to be the best." She paused, wiped her eyes with a tissue. "Practice sessions were before school, after school, and weekends. I didn't understand how or why he was doing this at first. I mean, teachers don't pull in the big bucks, and he only charged my parents for the weekend sessions. I was taking up almost as much time as his full-time teaching job did. But I was naïve, I thought if I was good enough, accomplished enough, he would be the man who got me there, and fame and money may come with it. Looking back, it's pathetic really. For me to think I was so . . . important."

"No," Michelle chimed in. "It's not your fault. Predators seek prey. That's their DNA structure. It's not your weakness. It's his force of conviction. They must seek out victims. They must molest, rape, abuse, victimize. It is what they are programmed to do." There was much voracity in her voice. Michelle clearly had strong feelings about this. Melisa wondered if Dr. Schwartz had learned any of this in his psych rotations in medical school. Was what she was saying true? It sure seemed that way. Ricardo and Edgar sure seemed to have this behavior built into their genes.

"Go on, Brianna," Michelle encouraged.

"So, one day there was news that there was a recital in Kansas City. Judges and scouts from major schools and touring companies would be in attendance. The best classical guitar students in the country were invited and I was one of them. It was a two-day event, and we would be staying in a hotel for two nights. I was to play Brahms's Concerto in A Major. One of the toughest, most technical pieces ever written. But if I played beautifully enough, I would be a shoo-in at Juilliard at a minimum. Maybe even a scholarship. This was my chance. My big break.

"I was nervous but confident. My parents were thrilled. When Mr. Poe—sorry, when my teacher and I arrived in Kansas City, we checked into the Marriott Hotel on the Plaza. Separate rooms. He said that the school had paid for my expenses. I would find out later that my high school didn't even sanction the trip due to lack of funding for the arts. I was so stupid, I never even asked anyone at the school. Not my other teachers, whose classes I would be missing that Friday."

Brianna's mom started sobbing with her hands hiding her face. I'm sure she felt so guilty and horrible for what we were about to hear.

"He knocked on my door shortly after check-in," Brianna continued. "He said that I needed a massage to loosen up and relax before my performance. He started rubbing my shoulders and my back. He then unhooked my bra and started massaging my breasts, saying something about loosening the pectoral muscles. I was scared, but I had come so far in my training, I didn't want to make him mad. Before I knew it, he was forcing himself on me. At first gently, but then rough. It hurt. I was a virgin then. I bled. I cried. He finished and left the room. I just lay on the bed all night. In the morning, he came back to the room. He knocked on the door, but I only opened the door with the chain on it. My teacher said the recitals were starting and we needed to leave soon. I showered and dressed and left the hotel with him. I played terribly. I couldn't concentrate. I cried during my performance. We left the performance hall after my performance without talking to anyone. No judges, no other students nor teachers. It was like I never existed. We checked out of the hotel and left Kansas City to drive back to Denver. It is an eight-hour drive, and the only thing he said to me the whole trip was, 'We will have to increase your lessons if you are to recover from this.' He dropped me off at my house and drove away. He never spoke to my parents, never gave me any feedback about what I did actually play for the judges. He obviously knew it was his doing that made me fail so dramatically. The worst part was that I actually *believed him*."

Brianna spent the next thirty minutes describing a pattern of predatory behavior including repeated intimidation, manipulation, grooming, rape, forced oral sex, sodomy, and punishment. In all the years Dr. Schwartz had spent as a medical student, medical resident, and attending physician, he had only felt this nauseated one other time. That involved a very old man and a very determined urologist. The instrument used in that instance reminded Michael of a wire coat hanger with some type of spring-loaded dilator at one end. Brianna's story made him even more sick. The depths with which this man, this educator, went to, to chronically and sadistically torture this little girl made his blood boil and bile creep up in his throat. Schwartz felt weak, angry, guilty, and so sad for this girl. Brianna recalled the day that her mother found bloody underwear in Brianna's room. She wrote it off as her daughter having her first period even though her fourteen-year-old daughter had never approached her about it.

Bri's mom just figured that her daughter was embarrassed, as it had come so late when her friends had had theirs at twelve or thirteen.

Michelle finally asked, "Where is your attacker today?"

Brianna broke down again.

Her mother stepped in and said, "He got a reduced sentence for a plea deal. Since he was considered a first-time offender. He received a six-month imprisonment in a county lockup. Time served for an additional six months while the trial prep was going on. Five years' probation and he is still allowed to teach. Not in public school because he is on the sex offender's registry. But he can teach in private school and private lessons. He teaches private lessons in Boulder. I could scream. It is beyond infuriating. That is why Bri's therapist wanted her to come here to vent her frustrations. She has dropped out of school. She quit the guitar. And he is out there. This motherfucker is still out there. Living his life. Looking for his next victim."

Michael Schwartz took a deep breath, then stood and walked over to get some coffee.

————

Melisa did not choose to speak that night. She simply listened. To her fellow survivors, as they would now be known. All with similar stories. Similar depraved perpetrators. Melisa told Michelle that she would share next time. Hugs were passed around, and then Melisa and I headed for the door, in silence. I walked her back to the hospital's main entrance and told her that I would see her there tomorrow in room 402. She nodded and went inside. I veered off to the parking garage and found my car. The 2009 Acura MDX was showing its age. I climbed in and started her up. At home I wanted nothing more than to hear the sound of my kids' voices. I called my ex to see if I could pull that off. She answered on the seventh ring. "Shannon, it's Mike. May I speak to Madison or P.J. please? I know it's late, but it's been a rough day and I just need to hear them tonight."

"It's *really* late," she corrected. "Are you okay?" She feigned interest.

"Yes, I'm fine. Please, Shannon."

"Okay, just for a minute . . . you're on speaker, Mike." Of course, God forbid I spoke to my kids privately. But I would take what I could get this horrible evening.

"Hi guys! It's Dad. I'm sorry to wake you!"

"Hi, Daddy!" Madison said. "Hey, Dad," P.J. added, still half-asleep. "We miss you, when are you coming to visit us?"

"I'll see you guys so soon. I miss you so much. I can't wait for the three of us to go to Legoland again. I'll see you in just a few weeks. Be good, please be safe, and listen to your mother. I'll call you this weekend so I can hear all about school and your friends and stuff." I caught a small tear in my eye.

"We'll be good. I love you," Madison said.

"I love you more," I retorted. It was our thing. It used to be a family thing.

"Not possible," my little girl said and then hung up. I stared at the phone for a second and said out loud, "Possible, possible." This situation sucked. Big-time.

Sleep, on the other hand, was impossible. I lay in bed wide awake, thinking about how we can all live in a world, have kids, raise families. All the while pretending that horrors and atrocities so unthinkable are not occurring and these things can only be discussed in the damp, dark basement of a rundown church. These young people should be able to scream from the top of the Fourteeners west of Denver, scream from the gold dome of the state capitol building, "I was attacked, I was raped. I survived! I am here! And to those who promised justice and didn't deliver . . . fuck you too!"

I climbed out of bed. I threw on sweatpants and my slip-on New Balance sneakers and started wailing on the heavy bag in the garage until the ceiling beams squeaked and my wrists hurt. Exhausted, I pulled off the gloves, grabbed a La Croix from the fridge, and sat at my laptop in the living/dining room. I started looking up articles, situations, news stories. About abductions, rape victims, conviction rates, jail sentences, sex offender registry. Local here in Denver, other places in Colorado, other places in the U.S. I was reading about victims' rights, my dead sister's rights.

It was all extremely frightening and dissatisfying. These monsters were all around us. Blocks away. The worst of it was that was just who we knew about. Since most convicted sex offenders are functioning members of society with jobs, people who paid their taxes, there was probably less incentive to punish them long-term unless there was a public outcry to do so. It seemed that rarely happened. Many victims were the ones who could not rejoin their communities, rejoin society. Like Brianna.

I stared at the screen for a few hours until the sun started to creep in through the east window, through my shoddy and broken vertical blinds. The telltale sign of a cheap apartment. I'd get around to fixing them one day, I told myself. I set the Dell laptop to sleep and walked into the kitchen to make coffee. I missed my dog Cash so much at moments like this. My loyal American pit bull-Labrador mix was always up for a run at this hour. I lost him, like everything else in the divorce. A doctor does not stand a chance in a divorce. Sure, maybe he or she makes a few bucks. The problem is everyone knows that our hours are long, and our attention is usually on our work. The lawyer representing the nonmedical spouse is typically a shark and can smell our fatigue. He is usually some asshole who didn't get into medical school anyway. You learn early in your career it is nearly impossible to be married to two things at the same time.

———

Melisa sat by in room 402 watching for Christina, the physical therapist. Christina had been working on Edgar's arms and legs. She had been trying to get them to move. His left side just lay there. His right side could move a little. But he was unable to follow any of her commands.

The therapist struggled with Edgar, grunting and breathing heavily as she tried to manipulate his near-lifeless body. He was cognitively impaired; he just did not understand what she was trying to get him to do nor was he able to execute it. Christina finally got him back into his bed, and she then turned toward Melisa and said, "Very little improvement, I'm afraid. He is still what we call a maximum assist. He can't walk, can't talk, can't feed himself. He may not ever get those back. The doctor will know more, but it's not any measurable progress. At least none that I can see. He remains total care."

Melisa smiled gently at Christina and said, "That's what I thought. He's right where I thought he'd be. It's been a few days now. I think this is Grandpa now."

She closed her eyes to pretend as though this news was devastating to her; inside however, Melisa felt free. Her monster was left impotent. Literally and figuratively, though penile flaccidity had never stopped him from raping her in the past. The lack of blood and oxygen flow to the brain would certainly stop him now. *Father Time, he's undefeated*, Melisa thought. *Thank you, God,* she added to herself.

Christina gathered her props—the rolling walker, four-pronged cane, PT straps, and belts—and excused herself. "Time for phase two of your rehabilitation," Melisa leaned over Edgar and said as the door closed.

CHAPTER SEVENTEEN

I GOT to work about six a.m., grabbed some coffee in the doc's lounge, and poured some probably expired skim milk into the cup. That served two purposes: making the coffee less bitter as well as preventing third degree burns on the roof of my mouth. I had other patients to see, and I needed time to figure out what I was going to say to Melisa Ramos. I needed to come up with a plan for discharging Mr. Shivers that she would opt for. So far, I did not have one, and I knew how smart and how determined she was.

I began in oncology. I had admitted a patient to that ward the day before. A demented woman who had been living with her elderly husband. She was malnourished and dehydrated. What was most disturbing, however, was the tumor, the size of a White Castle slider, growing out of her back near the second and third thoracic vertebral bodies. It was paler than her skin. It was mushy like oatmeal. If you turned out the lights to her room for a few seconds, then turned them back on, you would see the maggots scurry away back under the skin of the tumor. It was a large basal cell carcinoma that had necrosed her skin and penetrated deep into the muscle of her back. The maggots had been feasting on this rich spread of blood and tissue for months.

It looked painful and would need immediate surgical excision. I worried that in her malnourished state she would not heal very well, so I had been working with a nutritionist to try to buff her up a bit before I cleared her for surgery.

We see things like this sometimes. It is sad and it is frustrating. A great deal of the practice of internal medicine is. When I finished seeing Ms. Ruby, as she liked to be called, I left her for room 402. I knocked on the door and saw Melisa first. She looked very Zen, very peaceful. I pulled up a chair. "Well . . . where are we with all of this?" I have a habit of putting the patient, or their family, in the driver's seat sometimes. It helps get you to the end of the meal quicker. Always the elegant maître d'.

Melisa looked at Edgar's face, then slowly turned to me. "Oh, I've been thinking, researching, and planning. I have a bad feeling that Gramps here didn't leave me much in the will. I'm going to go to group again tonight. I'd like to talk tonight."

I sighed and said, "That's great, Melisa. That's the best way to start healing."

She stifled a laugh and said, "Yeah, I suppose you're right, Doc." There was something sinister in her tone.

I continued, "I'd like to go with you again. To support you while you tell your story. Mr. Shivers has been approved for Health North Acute Rehab. He's going to be transferred there tomorrow afternoon." I let that sink in. "He will be there for three weeks, then to a nursing home for the rest of his extremely short life."

Melisa closed her eyes, stood, and looked out the window. "So, he'll get away with this. With me. With the others before me. No one will ever know what he did."

I sat for a minute before I said, "He will indeed. Unless you come forward. I can help you do that. There's still time."

Melisa walked to the bathroom and closed the door. "Please leave. You can meet me at group tonight, but leave me alone now," she said from behind the door.

So, I left, unsure what she was thinking.

I got to the church basement about ten minutes before eight. I wanted to be early so I would see Melisa enter. I wanted her to see there were people who cared about her. Maybe she would change her mind and come forward. Tell her story to the people who could act. Tell the police. The FBI. She was not there when I arrived. I got myself a cup of coffee, silenced my cell phone, and took a seat near the ring leader's chair. Michelle was in her usual pseudo-beatnik wardrobe with a welcoming smile. The circle was full. Just then, Melisa edged herself into the group, scooching up a plastic chair.

"Welcome. I see many familiar faces. That's very good. Who would like to start?" she queried. Several hands went up among the circle of chairs. Melisa actually spoke up. "I would, please." Michelle nodded at her with her typical smile of encouragement.

"My name is Melisa." My eyes were glued on hers, but she never looked at me. "I'm seventeen years old, I think. I have been abused physically and emotionally since I was less than five years old." My eyes then wandered. I did not know until then that Edgar Shivers wasn't her first assailant. She continued, "My father left my family when I was about that age. He moved away. My mom did the best she could, but she would drink sometimes and would bring home men from the bars near where we lived. Strange men. Sometimes she would pass out, and then they would come after me. I tried to tell her, but she said we needed help with money and bills and these men sometimes helped. Then she got a boyfriend. Ricardo. He was around a lot. He would drink and he smelled like sweat and dirt and body odor. He would come into my room at night. He was rough and he would force himself on me. Usually he was too drunk to stick it in. So he would beat me with his belt. I decided that I had to run away. I needed to find my dad. Even though he left me, I still loved him. So, one day, I stole away to go find him. In a truck. I thought it would go to New Mexico where the truck was from, but instead it brought me here to Denver. I knew that I had a grandpa here. I had his address. I had to find him and see if I could live with him." Melisa realized that she was leaving out a large part of how she came to be here in the group. But the medical records said she was the granddaughter of Edgar Shivers.

"I went to the house where my family said he lived. He took me in. He wasn't nice to me, but he said that living with him was safer than living with Mama and Ricardo, so he let me stay. I didn't like it in his house. He would never let me go in some of the rooms like the basement. Not that I wanted to.

"I spent all of my time in the library. The one on Tamarac Street. Near Aurora. I read all the time. I did well in school back in San Luis. All A's. I thought if I could read and learn maybe they'd take me back into a school near Grandpa's house. Then maybe I could get out of his house. He must have thought that was my plan too. One day, he carried a large bundle out of the basement. I was about eleven or twelve years old. He left in his yellow car truck thing and was gone all day. When he came back, he smelled badly, and he was tired. He went to bed. When he woke up, he spent the whole next day in the basement. Cleaning it. I was scared. I thought about running again. But I didn't want to get sent back to San Luis." Melisa was doing pretty well with this version of her story. Only Dr. Schwartz knew the truth, and he was not going to correct her.

"The next thing I knew, I was in a basement tied to a chair. Grandpa came down a little while later and shocked me with some stun gun thing. A Taser. I was paralyzed. That was the first day he raped me." Melisa took a deep breath. Michelle sighed deeply in her seat. "I was in that basement for three years or more, I think. He raped me every day. Either with his penis or with the handle of a plunger. He would tie me to the chair or chain me to the wall with leg irons and cuffs. Four-point style. I would scream, but the walls were thick and he was always patching them up to make them more soundproof. He never talked to me. He never took me out of the basement. He brought me leftover food. He would make me pee into a bucket. If I screamed too much, he would dump it on my head. Then he would make me clean it up with a towel." She stopped again. Took a sip of water from a bottle. Then started again. "I think I was pregnant once. But I had a miscarriage. Probably for the best. One day I escaped. I ran down the street, and I found a police officer. He brought me back to my grandpa's house. He thought I was just a runaway.

"I remained tied in that basement until Grandpa had a stroke and went to the hospital. The people at the hospital told me to come talk to you all. That's why I'm here." Melisa looked around. Nobody said a word.

There was not a dry eye in the room, mine included. Michelle then asked a young woman named Angela to give the group some follow-up about her time away from her abusive husband. A man who apparently runs a hedge fund and then comes home and beats his wife. After Angela finished, Michelle let a few more veteran group members share some thoughts, and then she adjourned the meeting.

I barely saw Melisa practically run out of the room. She never even looked in my direction. This young lady was much more clever than she let on. The truth was she had run away from a life of desperation in southern Colorado. She only tweaked that slightly to explain that the man who tortured her was her blood relative as opposed to a predator roaming the streets looking for victims. Same story, different lead characters. One thing was obvious: Melisa Ramos had a plan.

———

Sleep was not happening. So, I went for a jog, blasted some Stevie Ray Vaughn on my iPhone, and felt the night air in my lungs. I could not get it out of my mind. This horrible man, and tomorrow, Medicare, your tax dollars and more, were going to pay for his stroke rehab. It was maddening. I tried to put myself in Melisa's shoes. This is what the victim wanted. For reasons unclear. But I was in no position to argue with her. She had made that very clear. I was determined to keep her secret if that was what she wanted.

I arrived at the hospital at 5:30 a.m. that morning. Got my usual cup of bad coffee and skim milk and went to the dialysis unit to see a patient I had been treating for kidney failure. He was about ninety years old. A bit too old for HD, as we call it. Hemodialysis. His life story was simply too amazing not to try to keep this man alive, however.

His name was Linus. Linus Smythe. He had been born in London where his father worked as an engineer. This man was primarily responsible for the design and construction of the Tube subway system there. When Linus was about five, he was glad of it too. The Germans had waged war on England, and by 1942 the Battle of Britain raged. The German Luftwaffe would carpet-bomb the streets and buildings every night and sometimes into the morning. Linus and his family had climbed out of the tubes early one day after a night of refuge there once the "All Clear" whistle had blown overhead. But the lookout corporal had missed one. In the smog of London's skies, a lone Nazi Stuka reentered her airspace. As Linus and his family opened the front door of their flat, the air-raid siren sounded once again. Before Linus's father could gather the family and get out of the flat back to the London Underground, a cache of bombs dropped on the streets of the neighborhood. One hit Linus's building directly, and the subsequent explosion took out half their flat. Linus, his mum, and dad survived the blast with minor injuries, but his seven-year-old brother was killed instantly.

"One second he was there, the next he wasn't. Dad gathered up Mum and me and ran for the street. No one knew the tubes better'n Dad, and he got us back down there."

Linus told this story so matter-of-factly. He remembered it all so well despite being ninety years old. He had survived the war. Working with the war effort in Britain as a child, he eventually became a civil engineer himself. He was hired by a fracking firm outside of Denver in the 1970s and had lived here since. His kidneys started shutting down about that same time, and now here we were.

The people you meet in this job are truly amazing. They are why we do it. And usually, they are why we cannot hold our own lives together. I hoped my two kids remembered me the way Linus did his dad. But I am sure that they do not.

———

Melisa had been watching the nurses work since she had first arrived at the hospital over a week ago now. She had studied their patterns, movements, timing. She felt like a bank robber casing the joint for a big heist. Which, in a way, she was. She knew where the Pyxis was, the locked cabinet that held meds, and furthermore, she knew the passcode for it. Anytime that many individuals need to use the same locked device, the code must be easy to remember. In this case it was 4 (for the fourth floor) then 9-1-1. The most memorable three digits in medicine.

Of course, each nurse has to enter his or her specific code as well as the 4911 combination. Melisa had learned that Edgar's nurse Kelly had chosen 0317. St Patrick's Day. Her favorite holiday. Kelly had divulged this through chitchat when Melisa asked an innocent, unrelated question when the two were standing near the device. That, and Kelly had written it on a piece of white tape stuck to her ID badge. Melisa knew that a.m. meds were drawn at 0800 and dispensed at nine o'clock sharp. Evening meds at 2000 and dropped at nine p.m. sharp. Like clockwork. At nine a.m. the nurses were always busy in the rooms; none were at the nurses' station then. No one noticed Melisa approach the med room, use the code to enter the room, then enter the passcode, Kelly's code, into the Pyxis keypad.

Melisa had learned from Wikipedia and a Physician's Desk Reference (PDR) she'd found at the nurses' station that the medication used in death row lethal injection chambers was potassium chloride. The same potassium we eat in bananas every day. A highly concentrated dose causes a disruption of the electricity through the heart muscle and stops it from contracting. Cardiac arrest. This is a painful event unless the patient or inmate is premedicated with morphine or something similar first. Melisa's patient would not have that luxury.

A doctor will usually prescribe about 20–40 milliequivalents of potassium chloride to replete a low level in a patient's bloodstream. Any more than that can be considered dangerous to give all at once. Melisa figured that ten times that amount would stop Edgar's sick, twisted heart in one push. She grabbed an 80-cc syringe from the supply cart and opened the door to the Pyxis, which had now popped open. On the third shelf, Melisa found the potassium chloride solution in a three-ounce glass bottle. She turned it over and pulled back the plunger from its hub in the syringe. She next attached a 16-gauge needle to the syringe and shoved it into the glass vial, draining all three ounces into the large plastic syringe. She was concentrating on the task at hand. So much so that she never heard the door to the med room open.

———

Melisa turned to see Dr. Schwartz standing at the door. He was white as a hospital sheet. He lowered his head and blinked for at least three Mississippis, then sighed quietly.

"How did you get in here?" was his first of many questions.

"C'mon, Doc, it's not exactly Fort Knox around here," Melisa said with a slight bit of arrogance she could tell pissed him off. "I've been living here for a week."

He opened his eyes. "Yes, I guess you have. I thought you might . . . try something like this."

Melisa was a bit puzzled but played along. "Why? Because you know me so well?"

He paused again before saying, "No. Because I know victim mentality. My sister was taken much like you were. Exactly like you were. She was only eleven years old at the time. I was seven. They raped her and killed her. Two men. And they got away with it. For a while anyway. One got caught and said the other was dead. We were not sure if that was true. There were conflicting witness accounts. The point is, I know what you're going through. And I get it. But you have your whole life to get through. This isn't the way. So, give me the syringe. Get out of this closet, go downstairs, and get yourself some coffee."

Schwartz held out his hand.

"You're not going to turn me in?" Melisa asked without looking him in the eye.

"No. You were lost, you thought this was a bathroom. Go. Downstairs. Get a coffee. Take a seat down there. Figure out where you go from here. Make some plans for your life. This man will never harm you again. I'll see you at group on Tuesday. Now go."

Melisa handed him the fully loaded syringe and left the med room. Before she did, though, Michael asked her, "Which patient did you order the potassium for?"

"Muñoz, Patricia. Room 416. Congestive heart failure. On diuretics."

Smart girl, Michael thought.

———

They say guilt is a wasted emotion. It is a bag of bricks weighing you down. You just have to let it go. Anger does not last as long. Anger gets used up. In a workout. In a screaming match. In personal improvement. Guilt, on the other hand, is like an occult malignancy. A hidden cancer. It starts small and unseen. It grows, sometimes rapidly. It eventually consumes you and takes over every aspect of your being. You can try to let it go, but you cannot. You eventually confess to your wife or husband that you have been cheating on them to alleviate your conscience. When you have battled it for thirty years, sometimes it gets the better of you. And you act.

First, I walked to the telemetry tech desk monitor and flipped off the switch for room 402. Then I walked down the hall. Like Jim Morrison. I came to room 402 and pushed open the door. I knew no one would be in there. Kelly had administered Mr. Shivers's blood pressure meds, aspirin, atorvastatin, Protonix, and enoxaparin already. She was probably in room 405 by now. The physical therapist, Christina, would start on the ortho unit because those docs want their patients discharged post-op first in the day. Since elective orthopedic surgeries brought in the money, these bone and joint docs always got what they wanted. Internal medicine didn't generate a revenue. We were the redheaded stepchildren of the hospital, and we were invented to save money, not make any. So, I was alone, literally and figuratively, in room 402, with Edgar Shivers. Status post CVA.

I approached the bed, making sure the shades were pulled shut over the window. I noticed that the telemetry leads were attached to his chest wall. Since I had turned off the monitor outside, no one would notice when I unhooked the lead cable from the battery pack that hung from a nylon bag around his neck.

I did not have a ton of time. I found the peripheral IV on his left antecubital fossa, his left forearm, and pushed in 10 milliliters of normal saline to clear and flush it. Mr. Shivers was sound asleep the entire time, as I expected he would be after he had been fed his breakfast a few hours before. I then took the 80 cc syringe with the potassium chloride, or Kcl, in it out of my lab coat pocket. Normally, one would get a morphine blast ahead of the Kcl even for a murderer on death row. Since this sadistic creature was now under my care, I skipped that step.

I slowly pushed all 80 cc, or milliliters, into the IV catheter, chased it with another 10 cc of the normal saline, and headed for the door, putting all used contents back into my lab coat pocket. It would not be long. Had I pushed the plunger down quickly, he would have been dead already, but the slow IV push would buy me about ten seconds to get away. I walked back to the nurses' station, to the tele tech monitor and flipped on the switch.

―――――――

"Why is the patient in room 402 showing asystole?" I asked loudly, staring at the screen. "What the hell is going on?" Loud enough for passersby to hear. I ran into room 402. I pushed the lead cable back into the battery. I slammed the CODE BLUE button on the wall.

"I need some help in here!" I screamed and started pushing on Shivers's chest, feigning CPR like they do on TV. Others started running into the room, including Kelly, his nurse.

"Dear God," she said. "What the hell happened?"

"I just stopped by to check on him, since he was leaving for rehab today. He wasn't breathing," I said with fatigue in my voice from the compressions. "Someone push an amp of epi!" I hollered to the group. "Rebecca, can you intubate?" I asked my respiratory therapist, who had been administering oxygen and was a whiz with airway management. "Kelly, please take over for me on his chest."

"Ok, people, listen up." *I deserved an Oscar,* I thought. "I'm running this. This is a sixty-eight-year-old male with a massive right-sided MCA stroke approximately seven days ago. No medical power of attorney, just a teenage granddaughter. He's a full code, but prognosis is extremely poor. Likely event would be herniating brain stem from increased intracranial pressure." Always good to have a story.

"Hold compressions. Let's check for a pulse," I added, tapping Kelly on the shoulder.

I knew that all the king's horses and all the king's men were not going to get this poor bastard's heart started again.

"No pulse," Kelly stated.

"One more epi, resume compressions," I said. "Let's go for two more minutes. Still asystole on the monitor without CPR."

I took one last look around. "That's it. I'm calling it. He's gone. It's 9:19 a.m."

CHAPTER EIGHTEEN

"THANKS EVERYBODY, NICE TRY," I said and patted a few shoulders. Since he had a massive stroke, no one in this room thought it odd that he arrested and died. Hospital administration would poke around a little, as would the physician peer review committee. But I was quite sure no one would suspect that the patient's doctor had murdered him. That was a new one. Around here anyway. Melisa, of course, had laid the groundwork. She waited for the tele tech to be on breakfast break, and I knew the unit clerk, who was supposed to be watching the tele monitor during said break, would have no reason to ask a doctor what he was doing at the monitor. She probably did not even notice. That was our habit anyway before seeing patients. Checking their rhythms. It was probably the perfect crime. Melisa had quite a brilliant mind for her part. I was experiencing a bit of an adrenaline rush from all of this, I am a bit ashamed to admit. This abomination was dead. Justice was served. Judge, jury, and executioner.

———

No one even asked me all day long about the code blue and

subsequent death. The patient was old-ish, he had had a massive stroke, and then he died. Melisa had been clever enough to take the potassium chloride from a patient who had been getting a great deal of diuretic, namely furosemide. It was common to give such patients lots of replacement potassium. The tele tech had not noticed the break in recorded heart rhythm, and essentially, we had gotten away with murder. The perfect crime.

I didn't know which scared me more: the fact that I had taken someone's life or the fact that I didn't feel the least bit guilty about it. The truth was, I had not felt so accomplished in fifteen years practicing medicine. Heroic saves did not compare to this. A demon had been destroyed. A monster slain. He deserved it, and I was honored to have been the one to do it. He would not be getting taxpayers to pay his rehab bills, for his nursing care, his convalescent home. Nothing. He would have a pauper's funeral, and then he would just be gone off the face of the earth. Only his haunting past deeds and sadism would remain. With Melisa. With his other victims. With me.

The truth was, in medicine we tend to get past our failed code blues and dead patients a lot quicker when there is no family to whom to explain what occurred. How we tried and failed. No need to figure out if the family is upset, angry, vengeful, litigious. Are they going to inquire about a potential lawsuit? Their nephew, neighbor, fellow church member is *always* an attorney, and even the utmost care gets scrutinized. Fast buck. That is why we do the best we can and document diligently. We are constantly protecting ourselves. CYA. Cover Your Ass.

It would never come, in this case. Obviously. He had no one. No one to question his death. Only those who would celebrate it. And those who did may finally sleep well tonight. I knew I would. For the first time in a long, long stretch.

———

I was off the next day. I had checked out all of my patients to Dr. Day, a colleague, and I tried to take my mind off everything. I awoke to pour and drink a leisurely coffee. I called Shannon and the kids to check in. They were all good. School, basketball, tennis, even surfing lessons. Maddie played guitar. Active lives. It would have been nice to hear a "Thanks, Dad" since I was footing the bill for all of it. But I was so relaxed that I did not mind.

After coffee I hit the gym. Hard. Free weights, resistance bands. Then I skipped rope for ten minutes straight and ran for four miles. It may not sound like much, but for a forty-something, it was pretty good, I thought. I felt young and strong. I went to the grocery store from the gym. My most hated chore. I stocked up on staples: deli turkey, oranges, grapes, green drinks, cereal, milk, frozen pizza, and coffee. Also a couple of twelve packs of La Croix. Tangerine flavored. Enough food to last ten to fourteen days. I ate breakfast and some-times lunch at the hospital. I lived pretty meagerly. With the excep-tion of child support and alimony, my cost of living was quite low. Denver speaking, that is. Probably not unlike that sick fuck Edgar Shivers. I was realizing that I could not stop thinking about him.

I left the grocery store after about eleven minutes. More time than I liked to spend there. I went home to shower and get ready for support group in a few hours.

———

Melisa was going to have to figure out her next move. She was officially homeless. She laughed out loud at the thought that Edgar Shivers left her in his will. *He did leave a vacant house,* she thought. One that never received visitors.

She grabbed up her things from room 402 and quickly left the hospital. No one even noticed or said good-bye. Once a patient dies inside the hospital's walls, they were largely forgotten. In this case, *Good riddance,* thought Melisa. She vaguely remembered where the house was. Holly Street, she remembered. About twenty blocks from the hospital. She felt she could walk it, didn't really have a choice. The sky was gray, a rare achievement in Denver, which was techni-cally in high desert. It was sunny year-round and rained rarely.

Melisa had a painful and horrific flashback when she was near the house. She had tried to block out most of what had happened while she was in the house, but she felt strangely empowered now that Edgar was dead, and no one was looking for him. The door to the house was unlocked. She entered slowly, half expecting some long-lost niece or nephew to come out of the kitchen wondering who she was. After several minutes of searching through Edgar's shitty, dilapidated house revealed no guests, it was obvious she was alone now. At least she found no other victims like she had been. Melisa came upon a guest bedroom with an adjoining full bathroom, and she figured she would call this her room for now. The electricity was obviously still on, and she surmised she had a month or two before Xcel Energy wised up and realized they would be getting no more checks from 1712 South Holly Street.

Melisa brought in the mail. She scanned the envelopes to see if any of them appeared to contain any loose cash, to no avail. But then, who sends greeting cards to a pervert? Clearly, no one.

Luck would have it that there was a washer and a dryer. She stripped and washed her clothes plus some other sweatshirts and socks and T-shirts she found in the dead man's dresser. She showered and changed. She found some Swanson frozen dinners in the freezer, and there was a gas oven in the kitchen. After picking at some poorly warmed turkey and mashed potatoes for ten minutes, she threw the tray away. It got to be around eleven p.m., and although she was quite on edge from being back in the house of torture, she was able to manage some sleep, maybe four hours' worth. She had her support group tonight, and she knew that Dr. Schwartz would be there. She had a couple of errands to run first in the morning. Or errands to walk, as the case would be.

CHAPTER NINETEEN

I GOT to the church a few minutes before eight p.m. I poured a coffee, stirred in some Coffeemate, and found my seat. It was hard to describe, but there was purpose now in my presence there. I was not a spectator. I was a participant. A silent warrior who walked the walk.

All day long I treat illnesses and deal with patients afflicted by them. Robin Williams famously said in the movie *Patch Adams* that if you treat a disease, you win, you lose. If you treat the person, you're guaranteed to win. I believed that. Or at least I used to. Oftentimes, you end up treating people because it is your job, or you're afraid of a lawsuit. Or you have nothing better to do.

Many of the patients we treat have brought their health issues on themselves. Never heeded the warnings of their family doc. Never attempted to lose weight or quit smoking or drinking. Or raping young women. What goes around comes around. There is a reckoning. I was starting to see.

Melisa came in and actually sat down next to me. She had on an old Denver Broncos sweatshirt, and she hadn't tied her hair into a ponytail. She looked like a soccer mom. Or a soccer older sister anyway who had just come in from Whole Foods. She seemed relaxed. She glanced at me but did not speak. Michelle spoke, though.

"Okay. Welcome back, everyone. I see some new faces. That's great that you've chosen to join us. To try to trust us. We are survivors. We are powerful. We gain power with each other's support. Who would like to begin?"

I glanced around. A girl I had seen there once before slowly raised her hand.

"I would, please." Michelle nodded at her warmly. The girl straightened up.

"My name is Alida. Alida Rivas."

Michelle jumped in. "No last names, please. Strictly anonymous here." She smiled again at the girl assuredly.

"I'm sorry. I forgot. I am used to saying my name. I had to say it to people so many times. The depositions. To the lawyers. The police. It's habit. My father was born in Mexico. So was my mother. My father paid a man—coyotes, they call them—to get them across the border. Into New Mexico. It's easier than Texas sometimes, less border control. A poorer state. My parents moved to a town called Hobbs. Near the Texas border. Oil country. Permian basin. But the oil money dried up, so to speak. There was no work there. So my parents traveled to Colorado. To Denver, to find work. There was supposed to be a lot of construction jobs. Soon after they got here, my father got cancer. He died when I was two. I was born here. My mother had to work as a cleaning lady to take care of me. She would work long hours. Long days. She would leave me with her neighbor. Her neighbor had a son. He was a teenager then. He would look after me sometimes. When I was about five, he started to touch me. Even though I knew it was wrong and it hurt and I wanted him to stop, I thought if I said anything, Mama wouldn't be able to let me stay there and she might lose her job. She had been through so much already. So I didn't say anything. By the time I was seven, he was raping me on a daily basis. I would cry and I would bleed. But still I stayed quiet. He told me that if I told anyone he would slit my throat and my mama's too. He left for college when I turned nine. He went to school in California at Stanford. That was eight years ago. He moved back here after he finished school and got a job. At a bank. The Great West Bank on Broadway Street. I saw his Facebook page. I wanted to throw up."

Alida held the hand of the woman next to her who was a blubbering mess by now.

"I told Mama about him last year. We went to the police. There was an investigation. Hence the lawyers and the depositions. But after many visits to offices and police stations they told us that there wasn't enough evidence for a trial. It was too long ago and they wouldn't prosecute this man. This banker. The police referred me to a counselor. She was nice. She has an office on Logan Street. She said that I would benefit from group counseling sessions. That I needed group support. So here I am."

The group clapped for her. I did some calculations in my head. Michelle continued speaking for a while, then dismissed the group for a break.

———

"Good morning and thank you for calling Great West Bank of Denver. How can we help you have a great day today? This is Marlene speaking."

"Well, hi, Marlene, my name is Stephen Francis. I was hoping to speak with the office manager about a personal matter," I said this with a degree of feigned enthusiasm into the receiver. Being a physician carried with it some acting skills, which translated well into daily life.

"Of course, my pleasure, I'll put you in touch with Glenn, our branch manager. Please hold." Marlene clicked over to the hold music. Disco today, it seemed.

As I waited, I double-checked my math, I needed to be sure.

The hold music switched from Thelma Houston to Bob Marley and the Wailers. "Stir It Up," one of the more tolerable Marley songs. *Oh, if you only knew, Bob, my friend*, I thought.

After about a verse of the song, it cut out, and an overly cheery voice said, "Glenn Watkins, manager speaking."

"Hi, Mr. Watkins, my name is Steve Francis and I appreciate you taking my call. I'm the chairman of the Stanford University Alumni Association. Class of ninety-one myself and I'm trying to track down one of our grads. He works in your branch, I believe. But our registrar's office lost his name. We just have his work address. Your bank. He would have been class of '01, I believe." This story was weak, but people love to be helpful when it comes to helping out people of authority.

I heard a slight chuckle on the other end of the receiver. "Oh yeah, of course. He has a flag on his desk with that tree thing, what do you call it?" Watkins inquired.

"The cardinal," I chimed back, playing along. "Big tree."

"Yep, that's it. Real bright kid. He talks about Palo Alto all the time too."

"That's him." I probed again, "Got a name? It's donation time again, I'm afraid."

"Oh, well, he probably won't like me giving out his info for a donation, but I suppose higher education has a price. Luke. Lucas Cranston. He's in investments and portfolio diversification. Big money. Does very well for us. He's at extension 5431," Watkins added.

"You, sir, are a prince. Thank you very much and have a glorious day." I hung up.

CHAPTER TWENTY

MELISA MADE a few calls to local utilities: Xcel, Comcast, Colorado Bell. She got her bills, Shivers's bills, extended by a month by claiming a death in the family. The house at 1712 South Holly Street remained alive.

She had been attending night classes at George Washington High School on Monaco Avenue. The principal there, a lovely woman, had informed Melisa that since she had attended Denver Public Schools before her prolonged "illness," as Melisa put it, her credits would transfer to GWHS. She was only two credits shy of her GED. Melisa would be eligible for the SAT and college admission. This became her focus. She was able to "borrow" some stationery from the school's administration office and had written herself some glowing letters of recommendation. Melisa's goal would be to enroll at CU Boulder or Colorado State University by the fall. Depending on her scores. She had been a straight A student before she was a prisoner. It was her escape from an unpleasant home life in the foster system. "Every book in the library" was her motto. She had not attained that goal, but she was damn close.

The staff at GWHS had been very accommodating. It was rare that they found a city kid with such ambition to do well. And the brains to back it up. Several of them had tutored Melisa after school and on weekends. Within the last two months, she had bolstered her GPA to a solid 4.0 with honors in three AP classes: math, physics, and history, her favorite subject. If she could manage to get a 1400 on her SAT, she would be a shoo-in for CU Boulder.

Now, if she could only figure a way to stay at Edgar's house a bit longer, she would put this place in her rearview and never look back. School provided breakfast and lunch to indigent students. Dinnertime and weekends were rough, but she had been managing. Odd jobs around the neighborhood allowed her to make a little extra cash.

There was one place to get some extra cash, she supposed.

———

Lucas Cranston was all over the internet. Facebook, Instagram, Stanford alumni websites. Apparently, he was a big deal there. As I searched the web, I wondered and strongly suspected that he had had other victims. How could he not? He was sick enough to be a kiddie rapist; why would he suddenly grow a conscience in a lush hunting ground like Palo Alto, California? He was a champion skier, was in the honors society, and had majored in business. The Great West Bank gig was probably just laying some groundwork before he entered the high stakes world of investment banking. He was apparently single, but looking at his Instagram revealed that he had had a series of attractive girlfriends.

I had the weekend off. Dr. Day was covering my pager. I had parked my SUV near the edge of the Great West service entrance. It was 4:55 on a Friday afternoon. *Almost quittin' time,* I thought. The window of my car had a tint. It was difficult to make out anyone inside, I knew. I was driving my own vehicle. Okay for short-lived recon missions but not ideal for actual work. I figured I could tail him without being spotted.

Lucas emerged at 5:05 on the dot. He sauntered to his 5 series BMW—probably a lease but good for appearances—then he hopped in. He took out his cell to send a few texts. Probably lining up a few honeys for the weekend. Then he started the engine and pealed out onto Colorado Boulevard heading north. The Friday afternoon traffic was thick and slow moving. We inched our way to Thirty-Second Street. He was in his Beemer; I was about three cars back. I did not know his address. It wasn't on any of his social media. That was the point of this, of course: to find out.

He took a left onto Thirty-Second at the light when it turned green, and he started heading west toward the Highlands section of Denver. The hippest restaurants and single-family dwellings were found here. Recently gentrified, of course.

He pulled into a spot on the street in front of 3255 Zuni Street. Grabbing a messenger-style bag from the trunk, he beeped the car locked and strolled into the building. From across the street, I noticed a second-story window turn on. Right on the corner. It was a nice building. Recently built. Three stories, studios and two bedrooms. Higher-end living. I assumed he lived alone, easier to find prey that way. He would probably have a few drinks in him when he returned here later tonight. He may or may not be alone. This might not happen in one try, I realized. If he were alone, however, he would have one guest he was not counting on.

———

I parked my black SUV about a mile from the apartment building, on a side street near Zuni. I had put my Trek mountain bike on the roof rack earlier in the day and was now bringing it down. Popped the front wheel back on its quick release and climbed on. I locked the door to the car and biked over to the building where Lucas Cranston lived. I had my supplies in my black North Face backpack, which matched my black- and navy blue-sweatshirt and jogging pants along with my black Pearl Izumi gloves. I would be difficult to see at night. Even the skull cap under my helmet was black.

Lucas never saw me approach him. I had been hanging around the corner of the building when the Uber he was in pulled up. I had to wait about an hour for him, but I figured the longer I waited, the more intoxicated he would be. He stumbled up the walkway and then stopped at the door to remove his keys. As he fumbled them out of his jeans pocket and inserted the right one in the lock, I trotted up to him and grabbed the door as if to assist.

"Thanks, bro," was what he managed to say.

"No, thank you, I have a Grub Hub delivery," I said, patting my backpack. He reeked of booze and marijuana smoke. Colorado's finest, I am sure. I followed him up the stairs pretending to be dropping off some Chinese food or Insomnia cookies. At the top of the stairs, I quickly scanned the hallway. No other people I could see. When Lucas made his way to his apartment door, I gave him time to open the door himself, and he had forgotten another person was still in the hallway with him. His would be the only fingerprints on his keys. Plus, I was still wearing my bike gloves anyway. As he pushed open the door, I quickly ran to him and placed the chloroform-soaked rag over his nose and mouth. We still stocked it in the hospital pharmacy, and a hospitalist's badge works everywhere to gain access in case of a code blue. I was careful to hold my own breath as I squeezed the cloth into his mouth. He bucked once, then collapsed in my arms. I gently pulled his limp body inside his apartment. No witnesses. No security camaras. The residents had complained it would make them feel like they were in a police state when the idea was proposed by the board a year ago. Whoops.

Now that Cranston was at home in his two-bedroom palace, I had to work quickly. I dragged his 175-pound body to his bedroom and lifted the pride of Stanford onto his California king. I removed my black backpack and took out an orogastric tube as well as a fifth of Stoli Vodka. I would need his blood alcohol content (BAC) to be over 400 during autopsy. That way, a presumed cause of death would be alcohol poisoning and maybe aspiration pneumonia, to boot. Not potassium chloride toxicity and cardiac arrest, which was what was actually going to kill him.

He was out like a light from the booze and the chloroform-ether mix, which I had read about on the internet, searching at the public library. The article said I would have about ten minutes before he may wake up, in the absence of alcohol, which was certainly not absent. It would be plenty of time. Once I secured the OG tube in place, I started slowly pouring in the vodka. I got the entire liter into him. He never even groaned. He was still breathing, though. I could hold his nares and mouth closed and suffocate him, but he may wake up. Young, otherwise healthy body may not give up without a fight. That could prove messy. I took the syringe out of my backpack; it had been preloaded with potassium chloride, two hundred milliequivalents. Probably a hundred would do, but I wasn't taking any chances.

Finding a vein wasn't easy; this guy was a bit dehydrated. I was saving him from a massive hangover. I found a vein that would be hardest to notice by the coroner at the posterior tibia. I entered it with a 20-gauge angiocath and got a good flash of blood. I hooked up the large syringe and pushed all 80 cc of fluid into the vein, then flushed it with 10 cc of normal saline. It drove the potassium straight into Lucas's heart.

I blotted up the needle mark. It was indetectable. The vodka was keeping him sedated and the potassium stopped his heart. I felt for a pulse in his carotid artery and found none.

Dead. It was 1:15 a.m. I gathered up all of my belongings. Standing from the doorway of his bedroom, Lucas looked peaceful. Later today or tomorrow someone would find him. Any autopsy would show alcohol poisoning. I quietly opened the doorway to the apartment and glanced into the hallway. I saw no one. As I made my way to the stairs, I was spotted. A young woman of about twenty-five was entering the stairwell from the bottom. She was probably just getting home from the bars too. It is possible she saw me leave Cranston's apartment. I had on my skully, bike helmet, and goggles. "Grub hub," I said, aware I must have looked strange in the hallway at night. "That guy was wasted. He will not even remember that he ordered tomorrow. Good night." I heard her giggling as I pushed open the door to the outside and exited the building. I found my bike where I had left it, climbed on, and sped my way back to my SUV parked a mile away.

CHAPTER TWENTY-ONE

MELISA HAD FINISHED her applications to the Colorado universities. She had nothing to do now but wait. She needed a few more weeks in the house on South Holly Street. She was low on funds, though, meaning she had none. While straightening up one day, she had come across a few hundred bucks in one of Edgar Shivers's bureau drawers, but that was long gone. She needed money. She also knew that there was only one person she could ask and that he would be in the one place she wanted to go least of all in the world. The past was the past. She simply wanted to move on. The group had served its purpose. She had closure.

As usual, Dr. Schwartz was sitting in the circle of chairs with his usual cup of bad coffee. When Melisa entered the church basement, he smiled his usual warm, professional smile. The group seemed larger tonight. Unlike the way Brad Pitt wanted it in *Fight Club*, people seemed to be talking about the group out there. Melisa had seen the movie on DVD in one of her foster homes when she was younger. The secret must be out about the helpfulness of this group, but more likely, or more sadly, there were more victims of sexual assault. Some statistics say as much as 25 percent of the female population may be affected. The group was growing. No one knew

Melisa personally, though. No one except Dr. Schwartz. She wanted to keep it that way. She didn't want to recognize anyone she knew. She didn't want to see anybody from foster care or school. Melisa felt safer when she was unknown. Anonymity was her friend.

Michelle settled and welcomed the group. Melisa took a seat next to Michael Schwartz. He seemed calm tonight, not anxious like he had been when Melisa first started attending the group with him months ago. Michael took a sip of his coffee. He did not make one of those gulping, gasping noises most adults did. It was nice. He smiled at her. It was not super friendly. It was more of the "sorry I just farted" variety than the "we're going to be okay" type. But that was okay. He never seemed creepy or romantic toward her, and that was good. She was just hoping he would seem more fatherly tonight as she had a big favor to ask. Melisa knew that she had about ninety minutes of group sharing to get through before she could ask him, though.

Michelle started. "I would like to welcome all of the new faces to our sexual assault survivors' group at the St. Pete's Church of Christ in the Mayfair neighborhood of Denver. We are always happy to have new friends, but we never want new survivors as it means new crimes are being perpetrated.

"I have news to share. Alida, it seems we have an update on your case. A man who fits the description of the man you had accused of your assault was found dead this morning. He died in his sleep. Drug overdose or alcohol overdose, they think. My friend in the Denver Police Department filled me in. Now, people, we need to remember that Alida had accused this man, but he was never convicted. Only suspected. While we survivors may sleep a bit better tonight, it is not our job to celebrate death while we search for justice. I just thought I'd share."

Michael glanced toward Alida Rivas and her mother who held hands and cried together. Tears of joy? Tears of relief, more likely.

"Now, before we have any new speakers, I'd like to take a few minutes to talk about what it means to be a survivor," Michelle continued. "Our lives are no longer in our assailants' hands. We are free of their abuse. Whether it was one occasion in our lives or an ongoing, recurring nightmare. We are free now. Free to live and lead our own lives. We do not find happiness in the pain, suffering, death of others. But sometimes in life, we find that sleep may come a bit easier after certain . . . developments." Michelle then looked at Alida and her mother. And smiled.

———

As the group was breaking for the night, Melisa found Dr. Schwartz at the coat rack. She approached him slowly.

"Good group tonight," she said emptily. "How have you been?"

Michael was pulling on his grey Mountain Hardware fleece. "Fine. Thank you. Busy, you know. Lots of sick people." He turned to face her. "How have *you* been?"

She managed a stifled smile. "Good . . . ya know. Trying to get back on my feet. I'm in school again. High school. GED classes actually. I just . . . finished. Night school. They let me slide on the course fees because I had good grades. I told them I had been sick, in and out of the hospital, so they didn't ask too many questions. I worked hard, so they were really nice and helpful." Melisa realized she was rambling a bit. Nervously.

"Melisa, that's fantastic. Great for you. So glad to hear it. What's next? Do you need anything?" Michael realized that he may not be the best person to get involved. He was the treating physician of her dead "grandfather."

"Funny you should ask, Doc." She then added, "Can we walk a bit?" She headed toward the door, not awaiting his response.

"Um, I guess we can. For a minute. I'm running late for a meeting, though." He threw that in to have an excuse locked and loaded. He followed her out the door.

Melisa knew he was not working that night. He would not have come to group if he was. She briefly wondered what it was he actually could be late for. His family lived in California, she had overheard him say once.

"Oh okay," she said hurriedly. When they were outside on the sidewalk, she started in. "I've been living in my grandpa's house.

Edgar Shivers's house. Lord knows he was not using it. I've managed to stave off the utility companies for a minute while I finished school. They were pretty understanding. My grandfather dying and all." She looked at her boots as if she was really mourning him. *Nice touch*, Michael thought. Convincing people.

"I've applied early admissions to CU and CSU. A few others. Fort Lewis College in Durango. But I need a bit more time. Until I hear if I'm in. The mortgage is due. He paid off most of it. There is some property tax and county fees. I'm not so worried about that. Let 'em foreclose. It will take months to settle that. Xcel is calling, though. I do need electricity and water. I use the internet at the library and of course no TV cable or anything. No extravagances. I'm broke, Doc. I have no way to keep the lights on. Once I get to school, I will move to Boulder or Fort Collins. I'll get a part-time job and apply for financial aid. But I need to be a student there first to apply. I'm not a minor. I need . . . I need money, Doc. Just a little. For now. I dunno, maybe a few thousand bucks over a few months. I know I have no right to ask you. But I have no one else. Can you help me?"

Michael stopped walking and looked at Melisa. She had an expression on her face that he had seen before. In the ER when he first met her. Scared. Beaten but not defeated. She was a warrior. She looked like he had looked so many years ago when he was a struggling medical student. Trying to pay the bills. Trying to do well in his courses. No one believing that he could or would succeed. Mortgaging his future with every student loan document that he signed. It was overwhelming and frustrating and . . . fucking scary. He did not know then if he was wasting his time. His "friends" told him he was not smart enough to get the job done. He had been scared. She looked scared now.

Michael did not give it a thought. He reached into his back pocket knowing he did not have any cash. He pulled out his worn Kenneth Cole wallet he had bought in Vegas one weekend rather than gambling. Inside it, he took out his red Wells Fargo debit card. He handed the card to Melisa and put the wallet back in his jeans pocket.

"PIN is 6847. Try to use Wells Fargo ATMs if you can. I hate that fee they charge you. I get paid every two weeks. It will fill up in that amount of time. Usually on Fridays. Take out whatever you need. There will not be enough in there to cover tuition. CU is up to about sixty grand a year for non-aid students. Anyway, when you get your first statement, come find me. We will figure out the best way to skin that cat. But this will get you to that point."

Melisa lowered her outstretched hand slightly. No one had been nice to her since she left Mama all those years ago in San Luis. A tear rolled off her nose onto the cold pavement below. "I don't know what to say," was her response.

"Don't say anything," Michael interjected. "Just study hard. One thing I've learned in academics, like sports, is you've gotta outwork the other guy. Or girl. No one is going to hand you anything and the world is unfair. The bell tolls at the university level for all those kids whose parents bought their way in. It's all about performance. You can be anything you want to be. Now go home. Get some sleep. I'll see you at group next week."

He gave her elbow a nudge with his bent elbow. And he walked away toward the hospital.

CHAPTER TWENTY-TWO

THE YOUNG MAN whom Michelle had introduced last night at group was not from Denver. He had grown up near Colorado Springs in a town called Woodland Park. It was a small mountain town with little social activity for kids, but they had a Boy Scout troop. The scoutmaster was retired Air Force. He had worked at the Academy in the Springs until he retired with full benefits and now was a successful defense contractor with a big firm. Billions. Between his full-time military duty and now as a scoutmaster, he'd had lots of access to young men and women. Impressionable young men and women who wanted to excel in life. Pleasers. This particular man, however, liked the boys a bit younger than those at the Academy. Eleven or twelve years old. Hence his involvement with the Scouts.

The first piece of information that I came across was from the *Colorado Springs Gazette*. It featured an article on a welcome weekend for the Church of Jesus Christ of Latter-day Saints temple in the Manitou Springs part of Colorado Springs. Charles Moore, the scoutmaster, was a deacon in the church. *Great,* I thought, nausea creeping over me. More kids with whom he could have potentially been involved.

The story that young "Jon" had told the group last night was the worst one yet. Or close to it. After weeks and weeks of stories I'd heard, that was saying something. Jon had been sodomized repeatedly by this guy Moore. Forced to perform oral sex. Since he joined the Boy Scouts at age eleven. His parents believed that scouting was the way to make a man of you. It was a very common belief among LDS church members. Almost all adolescents in the church were heavily involved in scouting. Jon was essentially forced to remain in scouting until age sixteen. Since Moore was a deacon and a prominent community figure, Jon realized that his credibility would not be questioned. He was a powerful man. Ex Air Force officer, rich, seemingly charitable with his time and money. The people loved him. The church loved him and his wealth. Seeing no way out, Jon ran away at age sixteen. He hitchhiked to Denver and had been living here since. He had made some friends in internet chat rooms and playing online games and had been staying with some of these friends and families in the Congress Park neighborhood in Denver. Not far from our church meeting. He had told the parents of his friends that his own mom and dad had been hit by a drunk driver and killed. He was reluctant to enter the foster system and also lied to these adults and told them his eighteenth birthday was only a few weeks away. If he could stay there until then, he would be free to pursue education and employment in Denver. They sympathetically agreed, but they insisted that he attend support groups for families of drunk driving accident victims. Jon agreed, and while he was researching those on the internet to look the part, he came across this group. Which was more appealing.

He had been in Denver now for three weeks. He'd last seen his own family at that time, but he felt glad to be rid of them. He believes on some level that they perpetuated his abuse by not noticing his depression and angst when it came to scouting. His reluctance to attend meetings and camping trips and hikes. Where most of the abuse occurred. Jon seemed pretty damaged by now. In need of a great deal of repair. Going to group was a good start. He would need a lifetime of therapy. The worst predators are the ones we are supposed to trust. The ones our loved ones trust as well. This Boy Scout troop leader was about as bad as it gets. Up there with perpetrators within the Catholic Church and Larry Nassar, the former doctor for the US women's Olympic gymnastics team. Also in Colorado Springs, by the way.

These familiar stalkers and predators destroy the credibility of their victims, which makes them feel that much more alone. When my own sister was abducted, there were hundreds of people looking for her. No one ever trusted her perpetrator. Not that we knew who they were. At least we knew from the get-go they were monsters. When it is someone the victim knows, it's that much worse. It boiled my blood to think about it. Obviously, people would be looking for Jon. His parents would have filed a missing person report by now and the search was on. Jon knew he could not stay in Denver forever. He would be looking to leave Colorado, maybe the country, until he turned eighteen and could change his name. Dye his hair, grow a beard. He was on the run. As the victim. Makes perfect sense. Ha.

After researching Charles Moore on the internet for a couple of hours at the Schlessman Family Branch Library, I headed home and went for a long run. Then I hit the heavy bag for thirty minutes. I had to work in the morning as well as all weekend. I would be off the following weekend, however. I called my ex in California before I left for the hospital so that I could talk to my kids. She answered and told me they were running late this morning getting ready for school. She put me on speaker phone, though, so I could at least tell them I loved them and was proud of them. I think they heard me. I hoped so anyway. Great bonding.

As I made a quick cup of coffee in the Keurig before heading out, I flipped on the kitchen TV to catch up on local news. The third story was about a banker from the Great West Bank in Glendale who had been found unresponsive in his apartment a few days prior. His name wasn't given, but the anchor stated that resuscitative efforts had been made but that the man was pronounced dead at the scene. The cause of death was believed to be accidental, and foul play was not suspected. He had been brought to Denver Health Medical Center for autopsy, which was ongoing. Just as I thought they would. I left for work.

CHAPTER TWENTY-THREE

JULIUS WILSON WAS a Denver PD detective with eighteen years' experience. He worked out of the Metro office at Fourteenth and Speer in downtown Denver. He was eating breakfast and drinking coffee at Pete's Kitchen on Colfax Tuesday morning. Going over his notes from the crime scene at the Cranston apartment in the Highlands was proving frustrating. A young man found dead by his landlord, who entered the apartment after a member of Lucas's ultimate frisbee team couldn't reach him after Lucas missed a game on Saturday morning. Since they had been out the night before and Cranston was excited about the game against LoDo, this seemed odd to the teammate. The landlord called 9-1-1 shortly after discovering the cold Cranston still in his bed. It seemed straightforward enough, but it still bothered Wilson.

Julius was just about to give up on it as a crime and chalk it up to natural causes. It had not been ruled a homicide by the medical examiner anyway. So it was not really a crime. Another entitled white boy who drank too much and killed himself. With six colleges in a fifty-mile radius, Wilson had seen plenty of that in eighteen years. Young man went out boozing. Drank his body weight in vodka. Locals had seen him at Lalo's and also at the Lucky Strike. He was drinking Kettle One and soda at one and Voodoo Ranger IPA at the other. Bad combination. High alcohol content in those. He was smart enough to take a Lyft home, the driver corroborated and witnessed him stumble into his building. The same address listed as his home address in his Lyft account. That was the last person to see him alive as far as Wilson knew. No video camera outside the building, as voted for by the tenant board. Case closed. Lucas vomited in his bed, aspirated his own puke, suffocated. Just like Jimi Hendrix, Julius's idol, had done in 1971.

One thing bugged him, though. A neighbor who Julius had interviewed said that she saw a Grub Hub delivery man come out of the hallway in the direction of Cranston's apartment. But there were no calls to any delivery restaurants on Lucas's cell phone history or laptop search history. Nor did any of the neighbors have deliveries at that hour. Furthermore, there were no cartons, bags, or containers from takeout in his apartment. It was possible it was just a foil or brown bag situation, as there were some of those trash items in his kitchen, but nothing looked recent. It was not unheard of, just odd.

There were no items missing, nothing stolen, nothing disrupted. No forced entry. Why would someone con their way or force their way into Cranston's apartment, see to it that Lucas died, and then leave? Everyone Wilson had interviewed or spoken with said that he was a great guy, nice, fun to be around. Happy. Went to Stanford and had come from a meager background in a modest neighborhood in Denver. Not a rich prick like so many other rich assholes we had in Denver, Wilson thought.

Julius needed to let this go. This poor bastard had drunk himself to death. It happened every day. Just like Jimi.

Let it go.

CHAPTER TWENTY-FOUR

I NEEDED to get some shifts at the hospital. I took in-house call every other day for about a week straight. The winter months were long in Colorado. Dry, cold, and dark. Lots of hospital admissions in those dreary days. Nursing home patients. The bread and butter of internal medicine. GOMERs, we call them in the business. Get Out of My Emergency Room. A term coined by an amazing novel written in the '70s. These are the bulk of inpatient medical service. Pneumonia, stroke, heart failure, urosepsis. These are the things most of us will die from, after we survive a heart attack or cancer, thanks to modern medicine.

I had admitted an elderly man who actually came from home, miraculously enough. He was only sixty-eight but looked 108 years old. Heavy smoker. Vietnam vet. Maybe Agent Orange exposure. On oxygen. He had heart failure from a bad mitral valve. Genetic. Mitral valve prolapse was the formal name. Once a doctor had told Mr. Spurgeon, my patient, that he had been given a bad heart by his mother. Mr. Spurgeon's response was, "If you say another word about my mama, I'll do you like I'd done Charlie in '68." Racial insensitivities aside, Mick Spurgeon won big points with me that day. His moxie. He had been coming to the hospital to see me ever since. He was not a candidate for a valve replacement surgery due to his poor lung function, so I tinkered with medications and other therapies to try to buy him a few more years. He spent them on his small farm just outside Denver's city limits. He was a retired cowboy, as he put it, and was surrounded by his horses and dogs all day. He was an incredible artist. Ink drawings of horses, birds, landscapes. Better than any of the overpriced, overhyped crap you will find in the galleries of Canyon Road, Santa Fe. I told him if I ever made it back down there, I would take a few of his artworks and try to sell them to the dealers there. He asked me how much they would go for. I said five thousand apiece easy. He drifted off to sleep that night with a big smile on his face.

I liked Mr. Spurgeon. I left him the next morning to see if I could get the case manager to get him some nursing help at his farmhouse. He did not have much time left. In any case, after about a week of making good at work, I'd earned a few days off. My Colorado Springs trip loomed.

Charles Moore was the thought that consumed most of my mind these days. I had checked out local motels that took cash, also campsites, even though it was February. I had memorized the locations and addresses of Mr. Moore's work and home and the Church of Jesus Christ of Latter-day Saints. It would not take me long to isolate him between two of these three locations. And I was to be a man in distress. Even though he liked boys, I was pretty sure good ole Charles would be available to lend a hand.

———

I left Denver for the Springs about three p.m. I wanted to beat the Friday afternoon rush hour traffic on I-25 south; that interstate was always undergoing construction. I never noticed any improvements in my entire life living in Denver. In any case I found a spot on the US Highway 24 spur. It took about an hour from Denver, and now I was pulling westward away from the Springs. Toward Woodland Park, Colorado. About a mile or two from Charles Moore's office park, where he and his colleagues figured out ways to screw taxpayers out of millions in defense bill contracts. I had chosen this spot because it was near his work and also on the way to the church where I knew he'd like to spend Friday evenings before heading home. The church was in Manitou Springs, near the Garden of the Gods state park.

I pulled over on US-24 and got my items ready. I'd been able to procure a bottle of ether from the hospital pharmacy. I'd signed it out with a scribbled signature indicated I needed it for some conscious sedation for a bedside procedure I'd be doing: abscess incision and drainage. Not the drug one would use for that, but everyone was too busy to notice. No one would bother to check. I'd seen this a million times.

I had another 80 cc syringe loaded with potassium chloride in my pocket. I would not need morphine or any other sedative because of the ether. I was wearing a black hoodie with Oakley sunglasses that took up most of my face. I had reached my destination on US-24. Previous recon trips down here in the last couple of weeks had proven that Charles Moore left his office at 5:00 p.m. sharp on Fridays. He then made a twenty-minute drive to the LDS Church in Manitou Springs to play basketball. LDS churches usually had a basketball court, I'd learned. These pickup games were usually participated in by kids after school, mostly boys, and they played until their parents could pick them up after work. Charles was on this, like flies on shit. Sick fucker. Literally.

I had changed the license plates on my SUV with those of an abandoned Chevy I had seen on I-70 near Commerce City a few days ago. No one would notice in the first place, but by the time they did, I would have put my regular plates back on the Acura. As the sun was setting to the west behind Pike's Peak, darkness was descending on US-24. This was timing out perfectly. At 4:55 p.m. I put on my hazard lights and raised the hood of my car. A man in distress. A car pulled over about a minute later. Not Moore's green Jeep Cherokee Sport. Damn.

The dad of a nice-looking family of four rolled the window down in their Volkswagen sedan. "Need a hand?" the man driving the car asked. The wife in the passenger seat smiled at me. I realized it was getting dark to have on shades, but I still needed them in the afternoon sun.

"All good, thanks. My buddy is on his way with jumper cables. Five minutes out." I had this line queued up.

"Are you sure that's the problem? Your blinkers are on. If the battery was dead—"

"Trust me, dude," I said. "This old beater needs at least twenty volts to start. I've been here before. But thanks for stopping." People in their forties did not like to be called "dude." I knew he would hit the bricks. And none too soon.

"Okay, well, good luck." The family man drove away. The little girl in the back seat waved to me as their Passat drove down the hill toward the Springs. Good Christian folk.

They were now a loose end I did not want or need. But hopefully the twilight hour, sunglasses, and fake license plate would exclude them from being a problem later. I thought about bailing for a split second when the Cherokee came toward me from Woodland Park. I crouched down over the engine block like I was prospecting for gold. The Jeep came to a halt facing me. He was now on the wrong side of the road. Clearly very eager to be helpful. LDS through and through. I heard the car door slam and his footsteps on the gravel. He approached me.

"What seems to be the trouble?" Moore inquired helpfully.

"Distributor cap popped off. I can see it down the engine block. I just can't reach it. I jacked up my hand trying too." I took out an ether dampened rag as if to nurse my wounded digits.

"Hmm . . . I think I can get to it." Moore leaned over and reached in. The smell of the engine was masking the odor of the ether. "I got it!" Moore said proudly. He popped it back on with his right hand. "How about that!"

He was basking in his victory as I grabbed his left arm with my gloved hand and with my right hand smushed the rag into his mouth and over his nose. He never even resisted. Total shock. Not used to being the prey, the sick fuck. Usually the aggressor. Typical bully. He went limp in my arms. I quickly glanced around. No one.

I popped the latch for the tailgate and lifted him into my SUV.

He was pretty light. About 160 pounds. But in my over adrenalized state, he seemed heavier. Once I had him inside the tailgate and with my tinted windows, no one would see him. I pulled two camping blankets over him just to be sure.

I looked around one more time. Carefully. I listened too. No approaching or leaving cars, trucks, or bikers. In Colorado, there is always one asshole on his Cannondale Carbon at any hour of the day or night. Except now. Good. I went back to Moore. Under the blankets, he lay breathing but not moving. Not much time. I found his external jugular vein on the side of his left neck and jabbed in all 20 cc, or 200 milliequivalents, of potassium chloride. Then I flushed the needle with 10 cc of sodium chloride to push the drug into his system. I checked for a pulse in his carotid artery and found none. His pupils were fixed and dilated. He was dead. It was 5:10 p.m.

———

The next part of my plan would take all night. I had to get his car and his body about forty-five miles southwest. I knew from my previous recon that there were two state troopers who patrolled this part of Route 24. One was on the west side of Woodland Park, and one was on the east side. This side. I had to move quickly. He would go to dinner soon, and hopefully the three bars in town would be rowdy at happy hour and keep him busy. I cinched my hood tight and got into Charles Moore's Jeep. I busted a U-turn and headed toward Woodland Park for about half a mile. Then I got out and jogged back to my car. I jumped in and drove it past the Jeep, for about another mile, and then parked it off the side of the road. I then jogged back to the Jeep and got in. I drove it about a mile past the Acura and then parked. Jogged back to the Acura then. This game of leapfrog was going to take about nine hours all told. I took breaks when the roads were pitch black and stopped to drink water and eat protein bars every hour or so. Once I got about five miles south of Woodland Park, where the mountain highway was barren and dark, I pulled the Jeep up even with my car. I then put Moore's body into it. Now, if I were in a pinch, I would just ditch him in it and drive away. He would be found, but it would buy me time to get away, and it would look like he had a heart attack or something. This was plan B. So far, Plan A was working, though. I kept up my little driving and running game. I was going to be very sore the next week or so. I was in good shape with all my jogging, heavy bag, rope jumping, and gym work. Hence this plan. But it was still a difficult one to execute.

I was moving at a pretty good clip. It took about three minutes or so to run the half mile back to each parked car and only a minute to drive up ahead another mile. After about fifteen miles it seemed as though I would make it easily to my destination by daybreak. Since this was a fairly rugged and uninhabited section of Colorado, there had not been a single car or truck pass during the night. It was windy and hilly, as the base of the Rocky Mountains tends to be. Even if someone had passed by in a car, they would likely have been more frightened of me than I of them. At night it would be very difficult to identify the make and color of two different SUVs on the side of the road, and a license plate ID would be impossible at forty-five miles an hour. All good, unless a cop happened by. So far, so good.

At 3:00 a.m. sharp I made it to my destination. Exhausted. The Royal Gorge near Cañon City loomed like an endless abyss in front of me. Similar to the Grand Canyon just southeast in Arizona, this natural creation was vast and deep. There was a suspension cable from which a large gondola hung, making it a fun family adventure. The gorge was several hundred feet deep and thousands wide. I rested for a quick minute in my car before driving it about a mile away and walked back to the Jeep at the gorge's edge. Charles lay lifeless in the back of the Cherokee. I reached into my pocket and pulled out the folded note written in black sharpie. It read,

I'M SORRY FOR THE PAIN I'VE CAUSED.

TO ALL OF THOSE BOYS AND THEIR FAMILIES WHO TRUSTED ME.

I'M SO SORRY.

With my still-gloved hands I placed the note inside Charles's shirt pocket and lifted him into the driver seat. The Jeep was on a nice little incline toward the gorge, and it was in park with the emergency brake applied. I released the brake and pulled the gear shift into neutral. I slammed the door shut and gave the Cherokee a little push. It didn't take much to get it going. After about twenty feet it neared the very edge and its inevitable plunge to destruction.

"So long, Charles. See you in hell," I said and turned to walk toward my car. I heard the loud tumble and scrape along the side, then the crash at the Royal Gorge bottom. Game over.

———

I got back to Denver in my Acura about 5:30 a.m. I was as tired as I had ever been. I took off every piece of clothing I had had on and deposited them in the dumpster outside the 7-Eleven at the corner of Leetsdale and Monaco in the Glendale neighborhood. No cameras outside the convenient store, which I had checked a few days before. I then drove home in sweats I had changed into back on the drive home. I was much in need of a shower and sleep. Charles Moore's body had been now in the canyon about three hours. Surely, he would been missed at Friday evening hoops at the church, and in all likelihood an early morning Colorado adrenaline junkie would have found him by now in the gorge. At least seen the wreckage and notified police. That was fine with me. I had not been spotted or caught during the trip there, and that was the dicey part of the excursion. If not, then his family—a wife and a daughter in college—would be worried by now and would have notified police that Charles never returned home after work. It was too soon for a missing person's case. It was six of one, half dozen of the other over who would actually find him now. Police or hikers.

It mattered little to me. Sleep came easily. Clear conscience.

CHAPTER TWENTY-FIVE

MELISA WAS BUSY. Good busy. She was attending full-time college courses in Boulder. Her scholarship had granted her a small dorm room to herself. That was good, no nosy roommate. In addition to a complete course load, she was working practically full-time as well at a restaurant called The Buff on Canyon Road. Good tips, good food. She was hustling all of the time, but it seemed to be working out. Campus and work were close. On her next day off, she was planning to take the hour-long bus ride back to Denver to visit the house on Holly Street, to do laundry and study. The utilities were paid there for the next few months, thanks to Dr. Schwartz and his magical debit card.

Life was proving to be difficult, but Melisa was determined to see this through. She had known for some time what she wanted to do with her life, and it was going to start with earning a degree and getting a high GPA doing so. Melisa had never been given the chance to excel before. She was determined not to squander it. She would awaken some nights in her room in a cold sweat with images of Edgar Shivers and his various foreign objects penetrating her. She'd then lie awake and tremble in the darkness, grateful that she didn't have a roommate to whom she had to explain herself. Sometimes it would take a minute to remember that he was dead and wasn't able to hurt her anymore. That thought gave her peace and motivation.

Friends were few and far between. She had little free time due to her studies and working at the restaurant. Once a month she had to meet with her scholarship counselor to prove she was attending classes and her GPA was solid. This was part of her academic full ride, they called it. That was usually painless. The other kids on campus didn't have her stressors. They mostly came from wealthy families in Colorado. They were looking to party mostly, and they were on a different track than Melisa was on. She had been a captive in a basement while they were experimenting on social media and were "liking" this or that. It seemed silly to Melisa. She could care less about posting things about her life for the world to see. She had a cell phone, which was purchased with Dr. Schwartz's card, but she didn't have any data plan with it. So, no internet. She just used it to call work or teacher's aides with homework questions. Occasionally, Michelle from group would call her to check in. This was usually frowned upon as the groups were supposed to remain anonymous, but Michelle explained that since Melisa was an orphan it was okay. Melisa did not mind anyway. Michelle was nice.

When isolation became a problem, Melisa would climb the bus from CU to Denver. She would look forward to seeing her cohort at group. They were a tight group. And as little as they actually knew about each other, they found strength in their bond. Dr. Schwartz was there sometimes too. Sometimes not. When he was, he always asked her about school and her classes. He always checked to see if she needed anything. She always said that she did not. He had done enough already. She wondered what he was doing when he was not there. She figured that the rigors of practicing medicine were a roller coaster. Likely draining.

It was nice to be with the group, however dysfunctional they all were. They ranged in age and degree of damage. Each story was devastating, painful. Incest, torture, beatings, sleep deprivation, food deprivation, cigarette burns, sodomy, oral sex, pedophilia. This list was horrifying. Somehow, though, in the midst of all of it, they found unity. Strength. Solidarity. Melisa yearned for a way to help them all. The victims. Heal the sick. Repair the damage. It became her obsession.

On some nights, Michelle would drive Melisa back to Boulder. They remained largely anonymous. Neither knew the other's last name. Melisa gathered that Michelle was single. Lived near Boulder. Maybe in Westminster or Louisville. In any case, it did not seem like too much of an inconvenience for Michelle to drive Melisa back to her dorm off Highway 36 in Boulder on the CU campus. They would only chitchat, never talking about the others in group or what was said. That would be frowned upon, of course. Michelle took her role as group leader seriously. She believed in what she was doing and didn't want to compromise her integrity or the integrity of the group. Trust was paramount for success, success in healing.

Melisa offered Michelle gas money, which she always declined. "It's my pleasure. You're a college student. I was, too, once," she'd say smiling. "Save your money for those Ramen noodles," Michelle would joke as she drove away.

———

Detective Wilson was in morning shift report, looking over some notes he had jotted down about an unsolved homicide in Thornton last month. A hit-and-run believed to be a DUI. DUIs in Thornton were the number one generator of revenue in that section of the city of Denver. On average, sixteen a day. Usually it translated into about $200,000 a day for that suburb and the lawyers around town.

In any case, Julius was lost in thought when the captain started talking about a suicide down near Colorado Springs, which had opened an investigation. A suicide note had been found in the vic's remains. The medical examiner in El Paso County didn't like the findings. Something about trajectory and angles. He thought a jumper would have made different numbers.

"Of course, this was Royal Gorge. Some two thousand feet to the base. How anyone can know anything about that, I have no idea," the captain said. "Anyway, the vic was a suspected kiddie raper.

Which he confessed to and apologized for in the note. Seems his conscience finally caught up with him. The detectives in the Springs want someone from Denver Metro in on this. For a second look. I need someone here to step up and take it. This case . . . it's a loser. Seems open and shut to me. No real upside. Scumbag is dead. Let's just leave him that way, right? But they're wanting cooperation on this from upstairs. So . . . who's it gonna be?"

Julius jumped up, knocking over his half-empty coffee cup and spilling its contents on his notepad. "Shit . . . I'm in, boss. I'm on it."

"Great, thanks, Wilson," Captain said halfheartedly. "Let me know what the ME says."

Julius mopped up the coffee spillage with a much too small napkin. *Something here just doesn't add up. Lot of that lately*, he thought and headed for the door.

———

I had unassigned ER call Saturday night. Lots of drunks and meth addicts as usual. A few nursing home patients. The kind of admission Edgar Shivers would have been had I not intervened with his outcome. He would have toiled away in some Medicare facility until he succumbed to one of several types of illnesses: dehydration, urinary tract infection, skin breakdown, malnutrition, fall, hip or spine fracture, or, most commonly, pneumonia. I spared him those, I guess. It is quite a life these nursing home patients lead. Or do not lead, as the case truly is. It did not really matter now. He was dead. I felt better about it. Good riddance.

Between Edgar Shivers, Lucas Cranston, and now Charles Moore, there were probably close to three dozen victims who would be sleeping better tonight. I finished my shift at 7:00 a.m. sharp the next morning. I hit the gym.

———

Melisa had studied for two midterms and worked a shift at The Buff that Wednesday. She caught the 7:15 p.m. bus to central

Denver by a second before it pulled out of the CU Boulder depot. She had just sat down to group as Michelle called it together at exactly 8:00 p.m. Glancing around, Melisa saw Michael Schwartz there. He looked well. Healthy, fit. Not like a lot of doctors who were pale and thin from too much fluorescent light and not a great deal of sunlight.

CHAPTER TWENTY-SIX

MICHELLE WAS INTRODUCING a girl named Dawn. Michelle hardly ever introduced anyone. It was anonymous. But Dawn's situation was special, and we were lucky she was there with us. Lucky she was alive tonight. Dawn had been the only surviving child of a family in rural Colorado where her father had been caught by her mother molesting Dawn's sister. The sister in question was seven years old. Dawn had been thirteen at the time. She was too old now for her father as he had moved on to her baby sister, Jill. When Dawn's mother, Katie, found out about his molestations, caught him in the act, she confronted him. The son of a bitch took out his Browning semiautomatic nine-millimeter pistol and shot Katie in the head, Jill in the chest, and then put the barrel in his mouth and squeezed. "By the grace of God," as she put it, Dawn had been at a sleepover party.

After the funerals, Dawn moved to Denver to live with her aunt, Katie's sister, who worked at the Whole Foods in Cherry Creek North. These group sessions were part of the family judge's mandate until Dawn would turn eighteen years old. Four years from now. Dawn's aunt, Jackie, was sitting next to her holding her hand. It was Jackie who was telling the group this story. Michael had a single thought apart from the horror story he had just heard: *One less for me to deal with.* He was refilling his coffee cup at break, and he was unaware that Melisa was approaching. "How are you, Doc?" she asked with her cheery smile. A rare sight.

"Oh hi. Good, thanks. Busy. Busy is good." Schwartz stammered these fragments out. Most health care workers said busy was good. Busy meant encounters, encounters meant billing. Billing meant dollars. Assuming the patients were insured.

Melisa leaned over and filled her cup from the Mr. Coffee machine. She poured in some Coffeemate, with a slight frown as she did. Who knew how long it had been sitting there. As she stirred her drink slowly, she said, without looking up, "I heard that the Boy Scout leader who had molested Jon killed himself outside Cañon City last week."

Michael looked at his cell phone disinterested. "Oh really? Yeah, I guess I'd heard about a jumper off Royal Gorge. I didn't put two and two together."

"Yeah. It was him," she said, though she knew he knew it was the same guy. "You mind if I ask you something, Doc? Why do you still come to this group?"

Michael thought for a minute, remembering that Melisa knew about his past. His childhood and the pain of his lost, tortured sister. "Well, I guess I thought it was very helpful to you. At first. And as your grandpa's doctor I wanted to support you. It slowly occurred to me that I had a great deal of anxiety and guilt about my sister. The survivors' stories help me to process some of that and channel it as well. It's a good place for me." He smiled at Melisa.

"Yeah, it's a great place. But maybe you should share next time Michelle asks for volunteers. I think you're starting to creep people out. You're always here. You never talk. Try it. It will help you." She walked back to the circle and found her seat.

———

Detective Wilson was driving on Route 50 west from I-25 toward Cañon City, Colorado. He had scheduled a meeting with the medical examiner of El Paso County. Passing the Golden Corral, Texas Roadhouse, Loaf 'N Jug, and Kum & Go near Pueblo, he was about fifteen minutes late. The municipal building on Main Street was pretty desolate. Two county vehicles in the parking lot. The ME was waiting for him in the lab. The body was still on the metal table. The funeral was being delayed, as there were questions about the manner of death. Charles Moore had certainly seen better days. The classic Y-shaped incision ran from both shoulders through the sternum and the abdomen. He was ashen gray. Julius choked back a gag.

"Detective Wilson," said the ME, Gordon, as he extended his hand. Julius reluctantly shook it.

"Thank you for coming down from Denver. The Broncos gonna be any good this year?" Gordon asked with a smile.

"Um, well, our D seems to be pretty solid, ya know. But we haven't had a quarterback since Peyton retired." Wilson managed a slight smile, but this guy just kind of freaked him out. Cuttin' up dead bodies all day.

"Yep, yep. Well," the physician began, "I don't think falling into Royal Gorge was this man's idea."

Julius took a slight step back. He covered his mouth and nose with a blue handkerchief he had pulled from his back pocket. "Why . . . what makes you think that?"

Gordon lifted up Charles's left arm. "The blood has pooled inside veins. Well, it had when I first examined the body at the site where he was found. Lividity, we call it. His heart muscle had died long before, hours before his body was found. And there was no bowel or bladder incontinence."

"Come again?" Julius interjected.

"He didn't piss or shit himself. The fall from the edge of the gorge to the bottom would have taken about four seconds. Never seen a similar suicide death where the vic didn't soil himself on the way down. Plus, he fell like he was spinning in midair, like he was limp on the fall. A man who decides to jump will tense up on the way down, will fall like a rock. Have you ever jumped limply from high dive? No. You tense as you make impact. Unless he was drunk, but we found no substances in his body. No alcohol, no weed, no coke, no valium. Nothing like that. The blood pooling and heart muscle thing could be explained by the temperature when he was found, which was thirty-nine degrees. But the whole story just does not add up. Now, this guy may have been involved with a series of sexual crimes. His note sure alleges that. Maybe he did have reason to off himself. Especially if word were about to break that he did all these things to all these kids. Those young boys. But I'll be honest with you, Detective. I have lived in this area for thirty years. I've never heard anything bad about this guy. Except one time. From an unstable kid who ran away. Maybe those two things are connected. Maybe not. Maybe the kid made up a story, no one believed him, so he split. In any case, in my opinion, someone out there knows more about this guy's suicide."

"Alleged suicide?" Wilson asked.

"I'm filing the manner of death as inconclusive as of now. Yes. Alleged suicide. It still just doesn't add up. As my wife would say, something she stole from Judge Judy, 'If it doesn't make sense, it isn't true.'"

"Wise women, both Judy and the Mrs.," Julius said with a half smile as he jotted a few notes on his pad. "Thanks, Doc. I appreciate your time." Wilson shook his hand again and then headed back to his Dodge Durango and jumped back on Route 50. Eastbound. Maybe Dickey's Barbecue Pit was still open for lunch. He needed to eat; then he needed to go over the interview notes of Charles Moore's family. Wilson needed to stop by Colorado Springs PD in their downtown office before he headed back to Denver.

———

Julius sat behind the wheel of his truck and finished off his Barbecue Pit iced tea as he reread his notes. It was discouraging for his current path of info. The interview with Charles Moore's widow and grown kids indicated that perhaps there had been speculation of wrongdoing on his part. Inappropriate encounters with boys both at the LDS Church as well as in the Scouts. His wife knew she should come forward, but she was concerned about their reputation as a family, in the church, if things came out. So she lived in denial. She buried it deep within herself. She was ashamed and was now seeking psychiatric help. She did not seem surprised that Moore killed himself. Part of her may even felt relieved, according to these notes. "Dammit," Wilson said to himself.

He had to find that kid who made the allegations before he ran away.

————

Back in Denver at Police Plaza on Colfax Avenue that evening, Wilson was looking up internet articles on Charles Moore of Colorado Springs, Colorado. He was, by most accounts, a fairly decent family man aside from what his widow, Shelley, had told the Springs PD. He was the father of two girls who were grown now. They refused to be interviewed. Moore was gainfully employed, a deacon at the Church of Jesus Christ of Latter-day Saints in Manitou Springs. There were raving accounts about Moore's volunteering, his dedication to the community. Hard work. A pillar. The article did mention, however, another side of the man. There was mention of one boy's name. A boy who had come forward, at first to his parents, claiming that Moore had been inappropriate with him while on Boy Scout expeditions and at church events. The boy alleged that there were other boys, too, but he refused to give names or dates. This boy's name had gotten out, though. It was Jon Agostino, and at one point he was even gave a deposition ordered by an attorney of some kind. There was talk a grand jury may convene in El Paso County. Possible indictment. But it never occurred. It was dropped at some point by the DA, and the boy allegedly may have recanted his testimony at someone's urging. *His parents? The church? Both?* thought Julius. Jon Agostino either ran away or was relocated by his family. He was rumored to be living in Denver now. *Denver, he was here.*

"Where are you hiding, young man?" Wilson said to himself. *Who is helping you?*

CHAPTER TWENTY-SEVEN

I WOKE up at two a.m. in a cold sweat. I was having a nightmare. I was a young boy, and I was running down the street chasing a brown van as it sped away, tires screeching. Black exhaust pumping from the tailpipe. My sister was inside screaming. Her screams became more faint as the van increased its distance. A faraway stoplight turned green, my last hope that it would halt. My little legs fatigued as they ran and my lungs burned. I could not go on. I collapsed on the pavement sobbing. Then I awoke. My heart was racing. Such nights were becoming a pattern. Sleep was evolving into nightmares. The only nights I slept were those when I had removed a monster from the earth. This was not a positive direction. I couldn't go on like this.

I peeled myself out of my sweaty sheets. I turned on the bedroom light and looked at myself in the mirror for the first time in a long time. I was on the fence between looking fit and looking gaunt. Like Christian Bale does in most of his movies. I had thin facial features but also the trace of a double chin that forty-plus-year-olds get despite the time they put in at the gym or on the street jogging. My hair was staying thick, not losing that yet, but it was turning grey. So was the wisp of stubble on my chin. Old. I was looking fucking old. Being a doctor makes you old. Being a parent makes you old. Being the surviving relative of a murdered sibling makes you old. I was all three.

I stumbled into the kitchen to make some Keurig coffee. My Achilles tendons were tight, and my left knee and my right elbow hurt. I was feeling that age I saw in the mirror. The coffee helped, though, and I made my way into the garage to hit the heavy bag for about fifteen minutes or so. Then I jumped rope for another ten. Then I switched back and started over. After an hour of this, a quick shower. Then I made a smoothie with yogurt, blackberries, blueberries, and a banana and got dressed for work. It was five a.m.

I had nine patients still in the hospital. I would be on call the following day, so I would double my roster—my census, we called it. Time to do some discharging. Getting people out of the hospital is by far the most satisfying part of this job. Once I had finished rounding, I had just enough time to grab a quick bite and then get to group. I had decided this morning at some point that Melisa was right. I needed to talk. I needed to tell my story. My sister's story.

I have grown in recent history to despise the term "my truth" or "your truth" or "her truth." This does a disservice to the word. To its meaning. There is "*the* truth," then a lot of versions of actual events. People have become so self-obsessed in our culture. It's nauseating. It detracts from those who actually need the focus. The attention. Even if they do not personally want it.

The air was chilly as I finished up a tuna sub from Jersey Mike's and started making my way toward the church on Clermont Street. I popped in a few Ice Breakers to mask the tuna breath. As I turned the corner, I noticed an unmarked police cruiser near the back entrance of the church. A well-dressed African American male, about fifty years old, was standing near it talking on a cell phone. There were no other cops with him. Alone, it seemed. He glanced toward me but then turned away. A good sign, I figured. If he had been looking for me, he did not act on it. Plus, I am not hard to find. I lead a fairly public life as a physician, as far as a Google search would reveal. I have avoided all social media religiously, however, as I find the entire concept appalling. So self-serving and egocentric. Nobody gives a shit what your sushi looks like.

I headed through the doorway and down the basement steps. I waved and nodded at Michelle and told her that I would like to speak tonight. I noticed Melisa in the circle as well. She looked happy, healthy. She had on a Patagonia fleece jacket and a Pistil skull cap. It was the look of someone who may be heading for the mountains of Breckenridge to ski after this. I hoped she was, for her sake. All work and no play.

Once Michelle settled the group, I noticed the police officer with a cup of coffee two seats over from her. That cannot be a coincidence. Two dead men, with allegations of abuse. But only one here in Denver. Edgar Shivers did not fit. He died in a hospital under physician and nursing care. So, I figured I was safe telling my story tonight. Good timing actually, as my victimness may exclude me from suspicion regarding these deaths. Michelle nodded at me. "Michael, would you like to start?"

———

I described in detail what an angel my older sister had been. Kind, polite. Would wear those barrettes with the skinny ribbons of two colors woven into them. She was bold, athletic, smart. Trusting. How? We could not believe it when the brown van slowed and snatched her. How they found her little body dumped in a wooded area by the street. Beaten, raped, tortured. I was a good storyteller, I suppose. There was not a dry eye among the group. But unfortunately, this story was true.

"They never caught all the guys who did it. Witnesses say there were two. One guy later was caught. He claims to have been alone the whole time. Says he stole the van. He died in prison some years later." I looked across at each person in the group. I saw Melisa wiping tears from her eyes.

Michelle wiped her cheek as well with a handkerchief. "Thank you, Michael. We know that can't have been easy." A slight reassuring smile from the queen of depressing tales. "Who else would like to share?"

After a moment, when I suppose people were gathering themselves, a young girl raised her hand. Just then a cell phone vibrated. A big no-no at group. This time was considered sacred. A healing time. The outside world was on hold. The differences made at group could be life changing for some survivors. Cell phone use was completely banned. The police officer, detective probably, jumped up to his feet and said a quick, "I'm so sorry," and headed for the door.

Good riddance, I thought. Michelle turned her focus back to the girl. She could not be older than thirteen. "Go on, dear."

"My name is Erica. And I'm a survivor. I guess." The crowd clapped briefly to show support. An unusual occurrence at group. When the speakers were this young, though, we tried to encourage as much as we could. Erica was holding a man's hand. "This is my dad. Henry." A few warm smiles. Hoping like hell he was not the perpetrator. "My parents divorced when I was three years old. It was difficult for me, even then. It was hard on my brother too. He was only two years old. My mom remarried. A man named Jim. Jim didn't have a job. He stayed home mostly, in my mom's apartment. He would sit on the couch and drink and do drugs. I was little. Maybe five when I knew what he was doing was bad. He was supposed to be babysitting me.

"My mom worked. But I didn't know where. Jim would touch me. He would tickle me sometimes. I didn't like it. He would try to make me laugh. Then he would try to get me to touch him. His penis. He would touch me with it. Try to put it inside me. Sometimes it would go in. It hurt." Erica began to cry. Her father began to cry as well. He squeezed her hand.

"Sometimes he tried to put his penis in me, but it was too soft so it wouldn't work. He'd get mad and yell at me. He'd hit me sometimes. Not in the face, so my mom wouldn't see." I looked at Melisa. She was closing her eyes. This asshole sounded a lot like Edgar Shivers, but of course, it was not him. He never had a romantic interest, it seemed. Just prisoners.

Erica continued. "Soon after that, other men would come over to the apartment when Mom was at work. They gave Jim money. They would touch me and put their penises inside me too. I would cry and scream, but they would cover my mouth. Sometimes Mom would come home, and I was happy. I thought she would be mad at Jim and make him stop. But she would just ask him how much money he made. If it wasn't much or if he'd spent a lot of it on drugs, she would be really mad. I would hide in my room under the bed. I tried to play with my little brother and keep him happy. He knew Jim was hurting me. He was scared all the time. We lived in a tiny apartment in Lakewood. Near Sloan's Lake. Jim could walk one block to buy drugs. One day he took too many and died. I was glad. But then Mom couldn't go to work because she had to stay home with me. She would have the men come over and see me then.

"I was eleven years old when a police officer came to the apartment and took me and my brother away. They split me and my brother up. I learned later he got sick and died at the Children's Hospital in Aurora. He was ten. He was with foster parents. Different from the ones I was with.

"One day a lady from the city court came and told me that my mom was in jail and that my father, who was in the Air Force, was coming home. To Denver, to stay." Erica looked up at her crying dad's face. "I was going to get to live with him. He was in Iraq in the war but was coming home now." She smiled at him. It was the most moving thing I had ever seen.

Erica continued. *Jesus, there's more?* I thought. "Mom was in jail for a while, but she got out. On probation. She's here in the city. In a halfway house. Just a few blocks from here. It makes me sick. She's that close to me. After all that she did. My therapist thought this group would be good for me. So here I am. I'm Erica. Thank you." Her dad squeezed her tight. Everyone clapped again. Most of us were still in tears.

I certainly had enough to go on. How many halfway houses could there be?

———

Melisa was studying for a statistics final in her dorm room when her cell phone beeped. It was Michelle. She was hoping to chat. The occasional friendly ride home to Boulder had evolved to the occasional chat. Melisa was fine with this. She did not really want it to go further from a social standpoint. Between school and work and group, she was spread thin and would hate to be a perpetual no-show at social events if they came up.

"Hey, girl," Melisa answered on one ring, putting down her pencil and pushing her desk chair back.

They shared small talk for a minute about her classes and about the restaurant and her workload. Making the Dean's list. Then Michelle got right to it. "Did you happen to notice an attractive black man at group last night?'"

Melisa thought for a minute. She chewed on her hair. She pondered answering in the affirmative versus pretending she had no idea what Michelle was taking about. "Um, yes, I suppose I did. Friend of yours?" Playing dumb. Usually worked.

"Well," Michelle continued, "he's a Denver Metro detective. Named Wilson. Julius Wilson. He called me ahead of time to let me know he'd be stopping by last night. He's investigating the deaths of Lucas Cranston and Charles Moore. Both had previously been accused of sexual assault. Both had alleged victims in our group—"

Melisa interjected, "Alleged? You don't believe Jon and Emily? They weren't alleged victims, Michelle. They are survivors of sexual, physical, and emotional abuse. You of all people should know that." Melisa realized she should have stayed silent, but her blood boiled when she thought of the perps. Those monsters.

"Oh yes, of course, I'm sorry. You're absolutely right, sweetie. I didn't mean it that way. The police jargon just kind of sticks in your head, you know. Anyway, speaking of survivors, you. Should we tell the detective about your grandfather? He abused you but then died before anyone could investigate. If he had other victims, committed other crimes, shouldn't the police know?"

Melisa had secretly been dreading a question just like this for some time. Maybe the state, the foster system, the university had looked into her past a bit. It was always a possibility. Even though she was sure Michael Schwartz would keep her secret, there were still loose ends with all of this. "Can I think about it, Michelle? I really . . . I'm not sure I'm ready to revisit anything again right now. I've made such progress. I can't go back there right now. Not right now. Please."

Michelle paused for a minute. "Of course, sweet girl. No problem. No rush. It may not be anything. I just thought of it since the detective was asking questions about the group's members."

"You didn't say anything, did you? The group . . . it's anonymous. Your rules. We have to be able to trust at least each other not to share secrets." Melisa felt on the verge of panic.

"Oh no! No no no! Never. He asked about members, but I told him the group was sacrosanct and that he would have to get names from another source. I assured him of that." Michelle seemed legit. Melisa was not sure.

"Well, I gotta get back to studying. I'll see you at next session."

———

I was making rounds the next day at work. I was checking on the progress of a teenager I had admitted while on call the previous night. He was thought to be about eighteen years old. We learned that he was Tibetan. The nurse and I surmised that he did not speak English, though he hadn't said a word since he'd been brought into the ER by ambulance from the street. His admission diagnosis was cellulitis with sepsis. He had multiple lacerations and abrasions to his back and buttocks, which were now infected. The skin infection, cellulitis, a subcutaneous infection, was probably caused by MRSA (methicillin-resistant Staphylococcus aureus). He would not talk to me through a translator, and this particular translator wasn't even sure that the patient spoke Tibetan, or Mandarin, or Hindi. This poor kid was despondent. He would just gaze out the window of his hospital room into the courtyard and the buildings past it. Not much of a view.

The injuries on his skin were clearly the result of physical abuse. Trauma. Over several weeks or months, judging by the extent. It did not take a genius (which I was not) to put two and two together and realize that this young man was being trafficked. Likely internationally. And somehow he'd made his way to Denver, Colorado. I tried to ask him about it. I asked through the translator, I asked when we were alone. I asked his nurse to ask him, too, when I was not around. I got Brandi, our social worker, involved. She is the nicest person in the world. He simply would not talk to anyone. We pleaded with him to let us help. Still no comment, no reaction. Just the gaze. Clearly PTSD. Major depressive disorder. I even tried to get him admitted to a psych hospital, but the chief psychiatrist told me that without conversation or willingness, he had no grounds to be involuntarily committed. Some system we have.

I spoke with a police officer at the local precinct over the phone. I got the runaround. No complaint, no investigation. The usual bullshit. It was maddening. I preferred my own "judge, jury, and executioner" model. After three days of intravenous antibiotics, this young man was ready for discharge. Brandi gave him all kinds of information, phone numbers, websites, and shelters. All local, not far from the hospital. Mission district. Stout Street Clinic. After his discharge, I found all these papers on his bedside table untouched. I hoped he at least found the eighty bucks I had stuffed in his jacket pocket. At least before his pimp did. This was the saddest part of my job. So frustrating. He was going back to the life.

CHAPTER TWENTY-EIGHT

I WAS in the doctor's lounge in the basement of the hospital. I was sipping coffee with skim milk in it and researching the Fox 31 Denver website for news stories. Particularly a story about a mother in Lakewood who had been pimping out her child. It may not be that rare of a story, unfortunately. But I had an approximate location, near Sloan's Lake, and age of the victim, if the Fox News people had their facts straight, which was a long shot. Either way, I may get lucky.

An overworked and exhausted OB-GYN resident physician named Stephanie Francis had not logged off from the computer in the corner of the lounge. Whoops. Michael Schwartz was now leaving no digital fingerprint of his search. I hated to use the poor young doc that way, but no one would be questioning her about anything, so I felt okay about it. I knew that I had not been extremely cautious with some of my recent "pursuits," but then again it was not a perfect world we lived in.

After about an hour of searching I located a story about young Erica's case. Her mother had been charged with child endangerment. Just that. The lone charge had been pleaded down from aggravated sexual assault, conspiracy to commit rape of a minor, sexual deviance, and forced sodomy. Those words made my stomach turn. Since the boyfriend, the initial assailant, had committed the initial and majority of the acts, Mom pled that she, too, was a victim. And because the asshole was now dead, there was no one to refute her but a small girl who had been traumatized. Not the best witness. The Lakewood assistant district attorney had dropped most of the charges, and Mom ended up serving six months in county lockup. Then moved to a halfway house to start over.

Grotesque. Some women and couples fight and struggle and suffer in order to conceive or adopt in hopes of having a child. This woman had two and then poisoned them with her selfish actions. My blood was boiling. I found her at last, though. Erica's story was true. Angie Truitt was living in a halfway house here in central Denver. Not ten blocks from where I was right now. There was even a photo of her, courtesy of the Denver PD. How thoughtful.

Melisa was in her dorm trying to cram for yet another final. This one was poli sci. A class that lacked excitement but was required for her major, so she needed to do well on it. Her previous exams had gone well: three As and one A–. That was in an elective, philosophy. Assuming she aced her poli sci test, she was looking at a 3.95 GPA this, her junior year. Her schedule was a bit off as matriculation goes. She had only been at CU for twenty-two months, but thanks to night classes, summer classes, and extra credits, she was looking to graduate with honors in just under ten months. Studying for the poli sci exam was not difficult, but she was having a difficult time shaking the phone call from Michelle. Why would the police want to hear from her now? No one knew that Edgar Shivers was not her grandfather. No one except Schwartz. Melisa knew he would never tell. She'd not only threatened him with HIPAA, but he was an accomplice. He was helping fund her education, for Chrissake, and he had never implied that he was bothered by any of it. Except her having to live through it. Could the cops be looking at him? Is that why she was potentially involved. Maybe how they met and how Melisa began coming to group?

Michelle had texted Melisa the cop's phone number. At 8:48 p.m., she could not take the suspense, nor the curiosity, and she picked up her phone and dialed the number.

"Wilson," the voice said after two rings.

Melisa paused and almost hung up. But her phone was not blocked. She would look silly and lose credibility if she bailed now.

"Um, hi, hello, this is Melisa. I got your number from Michelle in our survivors' support group. She told me to call you?"

"Oh yes, hi. Thank you for contacting me, Ms. Ramos." Clearly he knew her last name. That cannot be good. "My name is Julius Wilson, if you didn't know. I'm a Denver Metro detective. Homicide division." That bothered Melisa as well. Homicide implied people who died not on accident or from suicide. He continued, "I'm investigating the deaths of men who were alleged sexual assailants, or at least had been accused formally or informally as such. Both men, as it turns out, had victims, or accusers in your support group. I have been discussing this with Michelle as well as the MCPN mental health clinic of Denver, who oversees and subsidizes such peer groups. They can often be very plentiful with information when it comes to crime. In your case, it seems that your attacker is also dead. Is that correct? Your grandfather, I believe. I didn't know if you might have anything else to add about it. That's the reason for my inquiry." He stopped there. She was nauseated.

Melisa did not know how to respond, but she needed time. Lying to the cops was obviously a crime, at least if it impeded an investigation. Lying on a cell phone could haunt her for the rest of her life. She needed time. Melisa was a straight A student at one of the top universities in the nation, but she knew she was outmatched when it came to trying to hide anything from this man.

"I'm a bit uncomfortable discussing this over the phone, sir. There is a Java Hut coffee shop on Canyon Street in Boulder. Next to the REI sporting goods store and Wahoo Fish Taco. I'll meet you tomorrow and we can discuss this. Let's say 8:00 a.m.?"

"I'll see you then." Wilson hung up. Melisa froze. Should she tell

Michael? If so, how? Any call or text to him now could be traced back to her. Unless she used a public phone. She needed to find one. Quickly.

———

I was at the ICU Pyxis pretending to be getting out some lidocaine to start a central venous line on a patient. But I was actually loading up my 80 cc syringe with potassium chloride. Just then my cell phone rang. *Dammit.* It was a 303 number, one I did not recognize. A little late for a telemarketer. I was in no position to answer the call, not until I got out of the med room with the goods. My heart was racing as I finished up in the ICU and began my departure from the hospital. Ironic, given the meds I had just stolen were going to be used to stop the heart of a woman who had been selling her daughter's innocence and body for a few bucks. Selling her to buy drugs.

I'd forgotten to listen to the voice mail on my cell phone as I drove my Acura SUV west on Thirteenth Street and over to York to do a quick drive-by for a look-see. I needed to get Angie Truitt's routine memorized a little bit. A jogger would disguise nicely in this part of town. Close to Cheesman Park and a lot of young urbanites who stayed fit. I could probably run by in five-minute intervals until I got a good look at her. I had made mental notes, no physical ones, of her appearance and was sure I'd recognize her if I saw her again. Her arrest photos were, after all, only about six months old. She probably had not had time or resources to have any major plastic surgery or cosmetic work done.

I parked my MDX on Race Street near the park and got out with my running gear on. I had on a rain jacket, hood pulled, and Oakley Blades sunglasses. You would not have any idea that the post-call hospitalist from just down the street was now stalking his prey. While I had the syringe loaded and tucked in my zippered pocket, I was not convinced this would be the day. I had timed it perfectly. The sun was setting over Cheesman to the west, and it was harder to make out individuals specifically, but in Denver a jogger is never a strange sight. No matter the time, date, or weather conditions. Always some asshole running.

On my third pass around the side of the building, the halfway house, there she was. There was a covered porch, this was an old mansion really, donated by a philanthropic family for use by the city. It was grand, and the residents used the large wraparound porch to smoke and chat. All ex-cons on probation trying to start fresh. Angie Truitt was smoking a cigarette and speaking to another woman, who looked to be an employee of the facility or maybe a social worker. They were not interacting kindly toward one another. Not yelling, but not happy. I stopped to tie my shoe not ten feet from the pair. As I stood back up, the social worker left Angie and headed back inside. Angie crushed out her smoke and lit another. She moved forward and leaned on the granite railing. I made my move.

Jogging by slowly, I muttered, "Got some crystal. Good stuff. Cheap." I stopped and pretended to stretch my quad while she gave me a once-over. No shock, no surprise. She calmly asked back, "Got it on you?"

I switched quads and said, looking down, "I will. Five minutes. Meet me at the alley of Gaylord and Fourteenth Street." Two blocks away. I took off again, in the opposite direction of the alley where I would meet Angie Truitt. I made my way to the alley. I waited and pretended to be checking my pulse. Ten minutes, twenty passed by. She never showed. Cold feet, I guessed. Did not want to go back to prison. That was okay. I knew where she was now, I knew what she looked like. I knew she would be wanting to get high. Soon. I knew she was not going anywhere.

Patience was going to be paramount here. Not my strong suit. I ran around the park one time for good measure, then back to my parked car and got in. Angie Truitt, lucky girl. How long would her luck last?

As I drove away, I checked my cell phone. The voice mail message was from Melisa. She seemed upset about something. She asked me to call her back on her work phone at the restaurant after six p.m. It was 6:05 now. I punched in the numbers.

"Hey, Doc, how's it going?" Melisa was clearly nervous; she had never called me before. Our exchanges had been small chats at or after group but never serious and never over the phone.

"I'm fine. Thank you. How are you?" I was trying to be very formal.

"I'm great. They have those gluten-free enchiladas on special tonight at the restaurant. I'll see you at seven thirty. I got you a table. Bye." She hung up. It looked like I was driving to Boulder tonight. I was as ready as I was going to get, so I turned north on Colorado Boulevard and then on I-270 toward Boulder. Whatever it was Melisa needed to tell me could not be good.

I pulled into the parking lot of The Buff about 7:25 p.m. Luckily, it shared a lot with the Marriott Hotel, which made the area busy and crowded. Lots of people, lots of commotion. There was a line at the door of the restaurant; it was always crowded, especially when the weather was nice. I headed inside like I owned the place. Melisa saw me immediately and guided me to a two-top bar table. The crowd was noisy; there was a college baseball World Series game on the TV. Colorado State was playing Rice University. That may be the reason for the larger crowd. Maybe happy hour was still going on. Lots of Moscow Mule cups around.

"That detective called me," Melisa said first before I had even sat. "He was asking questions about Edgar Shivers. About group, about the victims of the other murdered men. I am meeting him next door at the Caribou Coffee tomorrow morning. He's going to ask me things. What do I tell him? What do I fucking say?" Melisa was terrified.

I thought about this for a minute. Then I took a sip of water from the glass the busboy had placed in front of me. I chewed the ice a little. Then I looked down with my arms crossed on the table. "You tell him the truth. Always. The truth. If he asks about Shivers's death, you tell him he had a cardiac arrest in the hospital. That's all you know. The doctors and nurses tried to revive him, but it was too late. That's all. You don't know anything else, and he can't prove that you do. If he asks you about the other men, you only say that you've heard stories in group. You do not identify victims. The group is anonymous. And he knows that. He can ask others if he needs to know more. He can talk to Michelle. Lastly, if he asks about me, you tell him the truth. I was Edgar Shivers's doctor. I asked you to attend the group as I thought it may help the grieving process. You had confided in me, after his death, that Edgar had been inappropriate with you. Which is why I didn't come forward. The man was dead. You found healing within the group. You and I became friends. My own kids were far away, and I was trying to help you. That's all.

"Melisa, you have too much to lose. Don't lie to the police. Tell them the truth. The truth shall set you free. You have done nothing wrong. You are the survivor. Stay strong. I'll see you later." I wanted to sit there in that restaurant with her for a bit longer. I wanted to reassure her that she was going to be okay. I hoped to help her be brave and get through this. But it was a bad idea for us to be seen together outside of group. And this meeting had gone on too long. I had to keep my worlds separate. I smiled at her as I walked out.

Julius saw Michael Schwartz leave the restaurant. He had noted the black Acura SUV in the parking lot even though Wilson had lost him on Highway 36 near Louisville. There was only one place he would be going at this hour. Wilson had Melisa Ramos's class and work schedule. It wasn't hard to put two and two together. So they were both in on this? Or just him? Julius would get to the bottom of it tomorrow at Caribou Coffee. It was getting late. The Marriott seemed like a good place to get some sack time tonight. He turned the engine off in his car and started walking toward the lobby.

After he checked into his modest queen single room, he poured himself an eleven-dollar Maker's Mark from the mini bar and sat down to go over his notes. There was definitely something here that he was missing. Were the victims in the support group hiring someone to take out their assailants? Why not just wait for legal justice? Stupid thought, since the conviction rate of sexual predators was exceedingly low. Lots of "he said, she said." They often walked. Especially when the accusers were children. It was a very dark secret of the legal world. Difficult to put these assholes away and even more so for anything longer than a slap on the wrist. When Julius's mother was sick a few years ago, before she died, her doctor said they were looking for an "occult malignancy," a hidden cancer, one somewhere in the body that was killing her, but they couldn't find it. Not the usual breast, lung, colon type of cancer but an almost microscopic one that was causing her so many health issues like weight loss, pain, confusion, infection. In the end, it was a rare lymphoma. It had been undetectable and only a clever medical examiner found it. In her abdomen. Julius had to pay $5,000 for a private autopsy to get this information. The cause of death was listed as natural, so neither the insurance company nor the county would pay for an autopsy. Great system.

In any case, hidden cancer was what killed his mom. No way to screen for it either, so Julius was at risk and would not know if he ever developed this illness. Until it was too late. These sexual attackers were like that, he supposed. They are hidden, in society, causing destruction, stealing lives, and leaving a trail of victims in their wake. It almost made sense, as the living victims met and shared their stories, that a fuse would be lit. A fuse of revenge. Wilson looked at the descriptions of the victims in the group. He had very few names because of the group's anonymity, but they were mostly young women and their friends or family. Some boys. A few men. Who would hire someone to kill these perps? Who could do it themselves? Were the survivors in on it together? That seemed unlikely. It was probably one or two acting alone or in concert. Small operation, little discussion. Mostly action. Two perps were dead. Perhaps by natural causes, suicide. Julius was under no direct orders from his captain to solve these crimes, if they could even be considered crimes; he was simply told to investigate any suspicious link between the deaths.

Had he done that? Could he let it go? These were likely bad men. They were dead. No one would lose sleep over it. As he stared out the window onto Canyon Boulevard below and all the college kids coming and going near campus, he poured another Maker's into his cup. He filled it with a little more ice and sat in the fuzzy chair with the worn ottoman.

Wilson made up his mind. He would talk to Melisa Ramos tomorrow at the coffee place. Get a few loose ends tied up. Then he would track down Dr. Schwartz at the hospital. Julius had the hospitalist's schedule and knew the doc would be seeing patients tomorrow. Not on call, just rounding. Julius would ask him a few cursory questions, make sure he was legit, and then he would close this case as solved. An overdose and a suicide. Done. *Let it go*, he told himself. He turned on SportsCenter on ESPN and checked on the Rockies double header score in Arizona. The fucking Dodgers were all but untouchable in the division anyway. *But we could still get a shot at a wild card spot if we could put together any kind of pitching*, Julius thought as he dozed off.

———

Melisa was a wreck as she waited for the detective. She ordered a small chai tea latte and sat at a small two-top table facing the door. Caribou Coffee was bustling at this hour. All the hungover college kids getting their triple shot espressos before their way too early classes began. In their world, 8:00 a.m. was too early. She fidgeted in her seat as she saw the large police detective enter the store. He gave a slight wave in her direction and then proceeded to the counter to order a coffee. He placed his order, a large mocha java roast blend with two sugars, and then walked over to Melisa's table. The drink would take a few minutes. He asked the young lady if he could sit, and she of course replied, "Please."

As he sat, Julius pulled a small faux-leather notepad from his pocket and clicked open his pen. "Thank you for meeting me, Ms. Ramos. I hope you're well." Slight smile.

"Well, you know, between school and work . . . staying pretty busy. I'm okay, I guess." Melisa was trying to nudge this meeting toward the end point.

"And your group. Your survivors' group. That probably takes

some time too." Wilson never looked up as he said this. "How well do you know the other members in the group?"

"We're friendly. I know almost everyone's first name, no last names. No addresses. Just their first name and their story." Melisa had rehearsed that answer.

"Except for Dr. Schwartz. You know his full name, place of employment. How is that exactly?" Wilson prepped his hand to jot a few notes.

"Julius . . . large MJ blend, two sugars," the woman boomed from behind the counter.

"Please excuse me." Wilson stood and walked over to the counter, dropped a dollar in the tip cup, and picked up his coffee. He took a small sip and then headed back to Melisa.

As he sat, she said, "Um, Dr. Schwartz was the man who told me about the group. He works in the hospital where my grandfather died. He was my grandfather's doctor. He died of a stroke a few months ago."

Wilson flipped back through his notes. "It says here that your grandfather died of cardiac arrest after his stroke. Dr. Schwartz was the attending physician and present when your grandfather's heart stopped, and he died. Is that right?"

"I guess . . . I guess so. I wasn't there. I think it had to do with the stroke. Heart trouble." Melisa took a small sip of her tea.

"And it was Dr. Schwartz who recommended the group to you. Because your grandfather was molesting you. For many years. He kept you prisoner in his basement." Wilson looked up from his notes.

"Yes. I thought there was anonymity within the group, but you seem to know things anyway," Melisa said, looking down.

Wilson chose to ignore this. "So your grandfather is dead. And so are two other suspected or alleged sexual perpetrators. From the group. Recently. That seems a bit coincidental to me. What do you think, Ms. Ramos?"

Melisa took a small sip again and sighed. "I suppose child molesters don't have the longest life expectancy. If you are willing to rape a child, maybe some of your other choices are poor too. Drinking, hard living, maybe underlying psychiatric illness. Depression. Seems to me."

Julius took a long sip of his cooled-off coffee. "I guess I can buy that, Ms. Ramos. Last question. Do you think Dr. Schwartz or anyone else in the group is capable of harming one of these types of perps? Killing them?"

Melisa stared directly into the detective's eyes and said strongly, "There is no doubt in my mind that each of these men died of natural causes. None of which were harmed by anyone I know. Are we done?"

"Yes. I thank you for your time. If you think of anything else, please let me know." Julius handed her a business card. He stood, waited for her to do the same, then he strolled out and left Boulder.

CHAPTER TWENTY-NINE

I HAD eighteen patients to round on that day. Four in the ICU and another five in the ICU stepdown unit. It was going to be a long day. I had been up since three in the morning, had worked out, and was fully caffeinated when I entered the hospital at 5:00 a.m. I was seeing my third patient in the ICU when I got a page from the hospital operator. I was a little annoyed. This patient was quite ill, on a ventilator and on pressors for life support. I was not sure what the source of the infection was, but her prognosis was grim. Her kidneys were shutting down, and I really didn't have time for an outside call. I spoke with the nurse about what our plan for the day would be, and I picked up a house phone and hit 00 for the operator.

"Schwartz, I was paged," was my usual response in these situations.

"Hello, Dr. Schwartz, this is Mary at the operator's desk. I have a call from a Denver Police Detective Wilson. He says he has some questions for you."

I was a little annoyed that Wilson was contacting me this way. Not a good look for a physician. "Um, okay, put him through, please." A few clicks and I heard his voice.

"Good morning, Dr. Schwartz. This is Julius Wilson from DPD.

We haven't formally met, but I'm investigating some deaths that have happened in the area. There are components of sexual assault. I know you attend the sex assault survivors' group at the church on Clermont Street. Any chance I'd be able to swing by the hospital and ask you a few questions today?"

I knew he likely knew my schedule, so lying about it was out. "Sure, how's lunchtime? There's a little deli in the lobby of the hospital. Let's say 12:30. How's that?"

"See you then, Doc. And I'm sorry to be interrupting your day like this. This info is time sensitive, but I'm hoping to close this case today." Julius hung up his desk phone.

———

Julius Wilson arrived at Rosie's Deli in the hospital lobby at 12:20 p.m. and saw no signs of the busy hospitalist physician. He ordered tuna on wheat and a La Croix lime seltzer.

As he waited, he pulled out his notepad and reviewed his notes from yesterday's meeting with Melisa Ramos at Caribou Coffee in Boulder. Her answers were spot-on like he had expected. Julius wanted very much to believe the doctor today and to file this case as "closed." That would depend on whether or not the answers Schwartz gave were in sync with hers and were credible. In the back of his mind, Wilson felt that these two could have been conspiring to commit murder. They had both been victims of sexual predators. Ramos personally and Schwartz through the assault on his sister who was just a child at the time. That *has* to weigh on you. Change you. Make you capable of doing things you would not otherwise do. It was an angel/devil on-the-shoulder situation. The angel on Julius's shoulder was telling him that the men who died were bad men and that this case needed to be over. Justice was served already. The devil, however, was wearing the detective's badge. He was telling Julius that something was not right here. The cop in him knew things were off. Who should he listen to? If Schwartz's answers were sketchy, Julius would have to investigate further. If he did not and more people died, how could he live with that? Even if they were bad men.

Dr. Schwartz trotted up to the counter Julius was occupying just then. They hadn't officially met yet, so Julius stood and extended his hand. "Julius Wilson, DPD," he said, looking the doctor in the eye.

"Hi, Michael Schwartz. Do you mind if we get right to it? Lot of sick people upstairs I need to get back to." All business.

"Certainly, certainly." Wilson sat back down and glanced at his notes. "Thank you for meeting me. I appreciate your time. Edgar Shivers was your patient, correct?"

"Yes. Very advanced stroke when he got here. Damage was done, I'm afraid," Michael said, quickly realizing he was violating HIPPA even post-mortem.

"And he died in the hospital after about five days? But not from a stroke?" Julius knew this answer too.

"He had a cardiac event, an arrhythmia and then arrest. It's actually one of the most common ways stroke patients die. The brain cannot tell the heart how to beat properly, so it short-circuits in a way. Shuts itself down. Not much we can do then. We ran a full code blue, but he didn't respond." Michael glanced at his watch.

Wilson continued, "His granddaughter. Melisa Ramos. You know her too. She was with him in the hospital. You encouraged her to go to your sexual assault survivors' group? She was abused by the late Mr. Shivers?"

"That's correct. I have a great deal of experience with these things. Professionally and personally, too, I'm afraid. I know that support from the local community is one of the best ways to heal from this type of trauma. She seems to be doing pretty well." Michael gave a slight smile.

Julius turned it up a notch. "Shortly after Edgar Shivers died, and shortly after Melisa Ramos started attending the group, two other men died as well. One was an apparent alcohol overdose. One was an apparent suicide. Both had been accused by members of your same group of sexual crimes. Not charged. Not convicted. But now dead." Julius took a sip of his La Croix. "Help me out here, Doc. Is that a coincidence?"

Michael Schwartz sat for a moment. He then said, "This is a highly unstable group of people. From a psychologic standpoint.

Suicide, substance abuse. Very common among both victims and perpetrators. I would have to say it is just that. Coincidence. These kinds of people rarely make it to an advanced age. One way or another, they oftentimes meet a tragic end. Depending on one's definition of tragedy. Anything else I can help you with, Detective?"

Julius stood again. "No, Doc. You've been very helpful. You have yourself a nice rest of your day. Good luck with those sick patients."

Michael left the deli as quickly as he had entered.

———

I finished my long day and headed home. I was exhausted. I felt like I had passed my inquiry with the detective. I needed to talk to my kids. I dialed the home number in California. My daughter answered on the third ring. I asked her to put the phone on speaker and get her brother. We chatted about school and sports. They were both tennis players and were learning to surf. I could hear them getting older. Growing into adolescents. It broke my heart, but it gave me hope. They did not have to grow up like I did. Nightmares about brown vans and my dead sister. They knew only loving, caring people. Their link to me was the only sadness they had to know. Shannon's husband seemed like a good man. They had gotten married not long after she and the kids relocated to Los Angeles. He had since provided a nice home for them. They were loved. Hopefully, one day I could see them again. That had yet to be determined, however.

I wanted to get my running gear back on and see if I could track down my friend at the halfway house. I knew I would not sleep again until she was dealt with. Her presence on this earth was a scourge, and I needed her daughter to have the peace of mind that this monster would never again harm her. I had on clean Pearl iZUMi running shorts, a jacket, and gloves. With a black beanie and Oakley sunglasses, I was essentially unrecognizable. I drank some coffee from my Keurig and packed the rest of my things, including duct tape and my syringe with the potassium chloride loaded.

The sun was setting to the west. I had to move. Now. I climbed in the Acura and headed toward the Congress Hill part of town. Near Cheesman Park. I found that High Street was practically empty of parked cars. I pulled over and put the syringe into my jacket pocket. Then I locked my car and started my run toward Thirteenth and York. The halfway house. I made it over there in about two minutes. It was getting dusky, and traffic was thick on York Street with everyone heading home from work toward Colfax Ave and I-70 to the north. As I turned north onto Thirteenth Street, I saw her. Clear as day. She was outside on the porch smoking. She looked haggard. Tired. Spent. I made one lap around just so she could see me. Then she may remember that I had what she needed. She was fresh last time. The risk was not worth the reward. Things were different now. Life was beating her up and she wanted to get high. I could feel it. I'd get her to follow me for a block or so. Down to the alley by High Street. She could not weigh more than 110 pounds. It would be easy to put her down with the chloroform, then get her in the SUV, plunge in the Kcl, and lights out. My heart started racing. As I made sure she saw me pass, I slowed to regain my pulse and breathing. One more pass and I'd stop by the porch. Stretch and see what she was into today. The sun was down, darkness filled the streets. I was in black. Practically invisible. Invisible to everyone except one other person I was not expecting.

CHAPTER THIRTY

DETECTIVE WILSON STOOD up from the stone steps leading to the porch of the halfway house at Thirteenth and York Street. He was wearing the same suit he had had on at the hospital about seven hours earlier. He looked like he had been sitting in this spot since then. I slowed to a stop about ten feet from him. I removed my Oakley Blades sunglasses.

"Edgar Shivers . . . owned a brown van." My stomach dropped. Wilson continued, "He and his brother paid cash for it. The title was bogus. It was likely originally stolen. When his brother died and took the fall for the rape and killing of a little girl on her way home from school, Edgar went on the run. His name was Acosta back then. Javier Acosta. He changed it to Edgar Shivers and got clean. Well, cleaner. He stopped using drugs, stopped drinking. Stopped robbing people. He got a job with a low-budget insurance scam operation out of Aurora. He learned the insurance business. Got pretty good at it too. Traded up. Found a company hiring in Glendale. Did well for himself. Bought a small house on Holly Street. He couldn't quite shake his demons, though. He would kidnap and rape little girls. In his basement. He used a yellow Subaru Baja instead of his van as he got older. Kids seem to like the yellow. I guess. He was at this for years. Dozens of victims. We've found the spot where he put them after he'd strangled them to death. It was up near Horsetooth Reservoir in Fort Collins. He'd pretend to be camping, then he'd bury them there."

I sat down on the curb. This information had blown my mind. The circle had become complete. My purpose seemed to have been fulfilled. In the most bizarre set of coincidences.

Wilson sat next to me. "After I figured out it was you with Cranston and Moore, I figured you'd be by here soon. I found her address from the Parole Board. I stopped by here a couple of nights last week. To check and see if she had any visitors. A woman staying here said a meth dealer posing as a jogger had spoken to her once. So I waited until that meth dealer came back. I knew who he'd be. And here we are. So are the toxic agents on you? Can you hand them over without me having to search you on this very public street?"

I stood and unzipped my jacket pocket. Handed the chloroform rag in a ziplock baggie and the 80 cc syringe over to the detective.

"Doc, you have the right to remain silent. Anything you say can and will be used against you in a court of law. You have the right to an attorney. Do you understand these rights as I have read them to you?"

I stuck my hands out to be cuffed and said, "Yes."

He led me to his car and put me in the back seat.

———

I did not say anything during my initial interrogation. I sat silently. The news had broken on the nine o'clock news that a prominent local doctor had been arrested on suspicion of two murders. One in Denver and one outside of Colorado Springs. Two professional men had apparently died of causes the district attorney was calling foul play. It would not be long before I was fired from the hospital, and the state medical board would likely revoke my license or at least suspend it by day's end. Until further notice. I had a savings account and a will stipulating that all my assets be left to my kids. Their new life was good, they would be fine. Shannon would hide them from this, and she could change their last name to her new husband's.

Julius Wilson was very smart. He had tracked my movements and schedule to look like a very good fit for the timings of the deaths of the two men. Edgar Shivers was not being listed as a victim. Detective Wilson and the DA were confident enough with the evidence they had for the other two that they felt they had their man. There was a witness, the family from US Highway 24 in Woodland Park who identified my Acura or a black Acura SUV anyway. Also the medical examiner in El Paso County who felt Moore's death was not a suicide. A witness from the hallway of Cranston's building in the Highlands who told Wilson she saw a person matching my build. This evidence was circumstantial, but it did not look good for me.

I didn't want to waste money on a high-priced lawyer, so I went with the public defender. I was not going to plead guilty, but I needed time to process things. At my arraignment, I took the fifth when asked how I chose to plead. The public defender wanted me to plead guilty to murder two, not premeditated. The Denver County DA wanted to go for murder one. Life in prison without parole. There was one piece of evidence that just did not fit, however. Motive. These were not random acts of violence. They were specific. These victims were in all likelihood guilty of sex crimes. A jury would almost certainly be sympathetic to the man who put them down. The DA knew this. Maybe a plea deal was possible. One that would put me away for a long time but not the max.

The judge had heard evidence, and a grand jury had decided that there was sufficient data to proceed with a trial. But they needed a plea from me first and I had not entered one. What was the judge gonna do, lock me up for contempt of court? That ship had sailed. I was probably going to jail for the rest of my life anyway. The judge had enough of my silence. He called a continuance of seventy-two hours.

CHAPTER THIRTY-ONE

I WAS BACK in my cell in county lockup. It was pretty awful. I was segregated from the other inmates as my status in the system was as of yet to be determined. So far I had managed not to interact with the other inmates. I passed the time by reading. They had a pretty good selection in the library. I found some Pat Conroy classics, which I'd read before, but it had been years. He is my favorite author. I was about halfway through the classic *The Lords of Discipline* when a guard opened my cell. I looked up.

"Schwartz, you got a visitor. Lawyer. Get up, follow me." He cuffed my hands and led me to the usual barren meeting room used for attorney meetings. Almost always a very unhappy place. An attractive black woman of about forty was sitting on the far end. She had on a power suit and had both a MacBook and a briefcase open. She stood when I entered the room. She held out a hand, and I did the same from my shackled wrist. We sat.

"Dr. Schwartz, my name is Anita Robeson. I'm a defense attorney. I am a founding partner in Waterman, Robeson, and D'Onofrio. We are a very high-priced firm in Boulder. Eighteen partners and twenty-two associates. Our record is unmatched in the

Rockies, and we only take cases in which we feel the defendant is being wrongfully accused. Or, should I say, accused of the wrong crime. You are wondering how I know any of this. We search the local law schools and colleges for our next associates. We've selected one for next semester. She applied to clerk with us then, and we plan on hiring her immediately out of law school. She has a 4.0 GPA from the University of Colorado at Boulder and scored a ninety-ninth percentile on her LSAT exam. She's been accepted to Harvard, Yale, and Stanford Law. She turned them all down to stay locally. She'll be at the University of Colorado Denver Law School on the Denver campus, and we are thrilled she will be joining us. Her name is Melisa Ramos, and she says you're not guilty. Not guilty due to reason of insanity. Post-traumatic stress disorder."

I was dumfounded but kept my expression stoic. Ms. Robeson continued, "I'm taking this case pro bono as I know you'll be in a financial hole soon. The bank will freeze your assets and your ex-wife will take the rest in alimony and child support. I've lined up expert witnesses in PTSD who specialize in the aftermath. The acts which the mind is capable of once it has been so badly damaged by psychological trauma. In your case, the abduction, rape, and murder of your nine-year-old sister. No one sought out counseling for you after that. You were forced to deal with it on your own. How could you? You were a child. You grew up with this horror and somehow made it all the way to your profession, a prominent physician. One day, the trauma came back, and your mind was forced to deal with it. It may have even been Melisa Ramos who triggered this. And you snapped. You had no defense mechanism ingrained, and as a result you acted out. You sought justice for your sister, for the victims you met in your support group.

"To me, this is open and shut. You are not guilty. I'm beyond thrilled that you have not entered a plea yet. With your permission I will enter this one for you tomorrow. I have a pre-arraignment meeting with the judge and the DA at 9:00 a.m. If I'm lucky, we can all agree what you need is psychiatric care, not prison. You may have to serve a few weeks until I can get the details arranged. Do you understand what I am telling you?" Anita Robeson closed her MacBook and looked at me. Dead in the eyes.

"Yes, ma'am, I do."

"Guard, we're all done here," Ms. Robeson said. She packed up her things and left with a smile. I went back to Carolina Military Institute courtesy of Mr. Pat Conroy.

EPILOGUE

THE NEXT SIX months were a bit of a whirlwind. I had to testify before the judge in an empty court without a jury. I had to tell my story again about my sister and her murder. The brown van and her captors. Detective Wilson had filled everyone in about the link between Edgar Shivers being both Melisa's assailant and also my patient, and how this started as a coincidence and evolved into a crime spree by me, based on the information I learned in a sexual assault survivors' group. No link was ever made between Edgar Shivers's death and my involvement. One that was pursued by law enforcement anyway. The expert witness psychiatrists from both Waterman, Robeson, and D'Onofrio as well as the state's own had listened intently. At the conclusion, all agreed that I was a classic case of PTSD and needed hospitalization for extended psychoanalysis and care. The judge sentenced me to the care of Sunrise Psychiatric Hospital in Englewood, Colorado, under the care of Dr. Robert Strickland. I was not a prisoner technically, but should I try to elope from the facility, I would be remanded to the State Psychiatric Prison in Pagosa Springs. Chance for release from there was doubtful. I had no plan for elopement anyway.

I was required to go to sessions three times a day. I was lucid and was not prescribed medication. I was allowed regular exercise and access to the library. The food was lousy, but I never complained. I had no visitors. I did not expect any. I knew people were separating themselves from the crazy doctor who had killed people.

———

At the six-month mark, the judge and Dr. Strickland decided that release was prudent. I was to maintain twice-weekly outpatient appointments with Dr. Strickland and check in with a state-appointed guardian weekly as well. I still had my apartment somehow, and my Acura was being released from impound.

I had obviously been fired from the hospital, but I had a hearing with the State Medical Board the following day. At the meeting, it was decided that I could still provide care to patients as a counselor. I could collect no fees, and my license had serious restrictions on it. No prescribing drugs and no billing insurance companies. But if I adhered to the guidelines, saw pro bono cases only as a group counselor, within five years I could begin a probationary position as a general practice physician again in a community in need. The state would appoint the clinic in question. Government wages.

I thanked them profusely for that opportunity.

———

I was getting dressed in my apartment. I put on a clean shirt and tie and had shaved. I definitely looked older. I was nearing fifty. I used to be forty-five and look thirty-five, but those days were over. I had heard from Anita Robeson. She explained that the families of Charles Moore and Luke Cranston could still come after me in civil court, and she had heard rumblings that they may. But since I had no money, they would probably hold off until I made some. Looking forward to that. I guess it is their right. Even though it seemed unfair. Therapy had taught me not to pass judgment. Not my job. I could only do what I could do in life, and I was grateful I still had some to live.

The group had gathered in the basement as usual. I saw several faces I recognized, including my old friend Melisa Ramos. She smiled at me. I knew that Melisa had tried to track down her mother in San Luis, but no one had seen or heard from Mama in years. She may have gone looking for her estranged husband; she may have died. Maybe at the hands of her abusive ex-boyfriend, Ricardo. I saw Michelle too. The younger victims in our old group had finished their required sessions if such sessions had been court appointed, as some were, and had not returned. Maybe they would one day. Maybe they would see the true value. So, I gathered the group together with a comment about taking your seats, and I began, "We are survivors. Welcome to our survivor group. Our community gives us strength, and we make each other stronger. For our newcomers, my name is Michael. I'm your group leader. And I'm a survivor. Who would like to begin tonight?"

AFTERWORD

All of the patients treated by Michael Schwartz in this novel were based on actual patients I have treated in hospitals across the country over the years. Even "Edgar Shivers." He was not a patient of mine in Denver where most of these other cases were seen. It was in a small town in another state. He was a federal inmate when I had met him. In that particular state, it is possible to go online and find out which crimes inmates had been convicted of committing. They recommend against that act, however. It is hard to stay free of judgment that way. "Edgar Shivers" had abducted and committed aggravated sexual assault on at least sixteen known underage victims. He was serving life without parole when I admitted him to the ICU for congestive heart failure. His CHF was quite advanced due to years of smoking, lack of exercise, and poor diet. Probably genes too. He did not know his parents. He may have been a victim, too, at one time or another. In any case, he died in my ICU that week from CHF despite our efforts to try to keep him alive as was his wish.

When he passed, the two armed guards who never left his room informed the prison administrators about the death, and Shivers was transported back to the prison morgue. Later, he was cremated. No one even knew. I felt sorrow. Not for him but for all the survivors he left in his wake. There was no one to tell their stories, to spread the word of his evil doings, if they kept their secrets with them. So the idea that they would all meet in a safe place to discuss the details of their stories, to heal themselves, was conceived in the author's mind.

They tell you, do not ever find out which crimes your patients have committed. Stay objective, treat the patient, treat the illness. That sounds great in theory. It is almost impossible to do, though. We are human. Humans have a curious nature. It got the better of us in the case of Edgar Shivers, as the nurses and I looked up his rap sheet on the Department of Corrections website one night. There were numerous articles in several local papers about him, too, eyewitness and victim statements about his heinous acts. You cannot help but wonder, "Why do I always have to be the good guy?"

That is where the seeds for this novel were sown. In the "What if instead of healing, I harmed? What if I sought justice rather than treated illness?" It seemed like an interesting enough topic anyway. This book is dedicated to the true heroes, though: the survivors of sexual assault. The ones who grow stronger, spread the word, and look out for one another. It is for them that these words were written.

Jim Steele, MD
    2021

ABOUT THE AUTHOR

James Steele, MD, is a practicing hospitalist physician. A hospitalist physician is an inpatient doctor who sees no patients in a primary care office or clinic. Only when hospitalized with a diagnosed condition which requires that level of care. Typical diagnoses are heart attacks, strokes, pneumonia, sepsis, and kidney failure. Dr. Steele has practiced as a full-time physician specializing in Hospital Medicine since 2007. Dr. Steele has worked in hospitals in eight different US States and continues to do so. He only half jokes that the Fox Network television show *The Resident* is loosely based on his life and experiences. Though he received no credit for this. Dr. Steele currently practices in his home state where he lives with his wife, two children, and four dogs. If he is not in the hospital seeing patients or working on his next novel, he can be found playing his guitar, Mabel, in his basement, snowboarding, playing tennis or listening to classic rock records in his garage.